Kate Fortune's Journal Entry

Oh, my! My son Jake accused of murdering Monica Malone! Whatever will the family do? I know, without a doubt in my mind, that Jake is innocent. That evil Monica has brought nothing but trouble for this family. I suspect she was at least partly responsible for my plane crash and supposed death. And I'm sure she wasn't acting alone. So, I must still remain in hiding to catch the culprits. But how am I going to help Jake get out of this mess?

A LETTER FROM THE AUTHOR

Dear Reader,

First and foremost, FORTUNE'S CHILDREN is about a family. A big, adventurous, larger-than-life and very American family. A family with a loving, powerful, matchmaking woman at its head. What fun, I thought, when my editor offered me the opportunity to write one of the twelve books in the series. I love to write about families. So I was hooked.

But there was more: an ongoing mystery revolving around that loving, powerful, matchmaking woman at the head of the family.

And *then* my editor told me about the other authors who'd be participating: really terrific award-winning, top-selling authors. I'd be in such good company.

And best of all, my own contribution to the series would include a sexy single dad, an adorable lost little boy, a Saint Bernard dog with a heart as big as Lake Superior—and a woman on the verge of a whole new life.

I mean, honestly. How could I resist?

I couldn't. And I didn't. And it's been every bit as much fun as I thought it would be.

I hope you enjoy *Wife Wanted*, too—as well as all the other books in the FORTUNE'S CHILDREN series.

Sincerely,

Christine Rimmer

Wife Wanted
CHRISTINE RIMMER

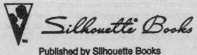

Silhouette Books

Published by Silhouette Books

America's Publisher of Contemporary Romance

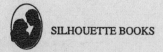

SILHOUETTE BOOKS

WIFE WANTED

Copyright © 1997 by Harlequin Books S.A.

ISBN 0-373-50184-6

Special thanks and acknowledgment to Christine Rimmer for her contribution to the Fortune's Children series.

Printed in U.S.A.

CHRISTINE RIMMER

is a third-generation Californian who came to her profession the long way around. Before settling down to write about the magic of romance, she'd been an actress, a salesclerk, a janitor, a model, a phone sales representative, a teacher, a waitress, a playwright and an office manager. Now that she's finally found work that suits her perfectly, she insists she never had a problem keeping a job—she was merely gaining "life experience" for her future as a novelist. Those who know her best withhold comment when she makes such claims; they are grateful that she's at last found steady work. Christine is grateful, too—not only for the joy she finds in writing, but for what waits when the day's work is through: a man she loves who loves her right back and the privilege of watching their children grow and change day to day.

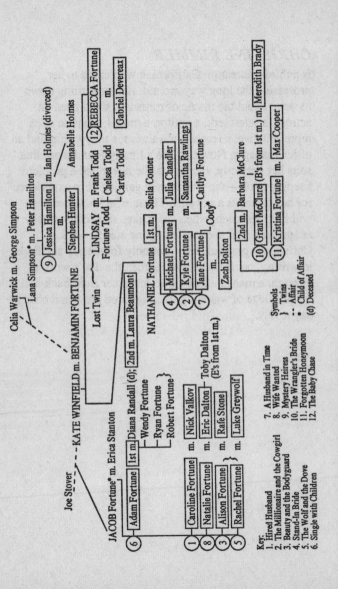

Key:
1. Hired Husband
2. The Millionaire and the Cowgirl
3. Beauty and the Bodyguard
4. Stand-In Bride
5. The Wolf and the Dove
6. Single with Children
7. A Husband in Time
8. Wife Wanted
9. Mystery Heiress
10. The Wrangler's Bride
11. Forgotten Honeymoon
12. The Baby Chase

Symbols
} Twins
-- Affair
• Child of Affair
(d) Deceased

F RTUNE'S
Children

Meet the Fortunes—three generations of a family with a legacy of wealth, influence and power. As they unite to face an unknown enemy, shocking family secrets are revealed...and passionate new romances are ignited.

NATALIE FORTUNE: The loving schoolteacher always helps those in need. However, an accident forces her to rely on her new tenant to care for her. And she soon finds that Eric Dalton's tender touch is irresistible....

ERIC DALTON: The handsome single father can't ignore the place Natalie has taken in his and his son's hearts. He is falling in love with her, but is he willing to take a risk on marriage and make Natalie his wife...?

JAKE FORTUNE: Will he stand idly by and let Monica Malone take over Fortune Cosmetics? Or will he find a way to stop Monica—permanently?

JESSICA HOLMES: This desperate mother needs help to save her young daughter's life. Will her newly found Fortune relatives come to her aid?

LIZ JONES—
CELEBRITY GOSSIP

Monica Malone is dead! And Jake Fortune is the murderer! Yeah, yeah, he says he's innocent. But come on, Jake. Weren't *you* the last one to see her alive? Weren't *you* arguing with her over a very personal— or perhaps financial— matter? Didn't your own daughter see *you* drunk, and disheveled?

And you expect the good people of this fine city to believe you're innocent? If you're not guilty, then I'm Princess Di!

I'm sick and tired of the rich and their fancy, high-priced lawyers getting away with murder— literally. I hope they throw the book at you, Jake Fortune!

One

The ad in the *Star Tribune* had sounded like just what the doctor ordered:

Last-Minute Summer Rental: Spacious, comfy farm-style lakefront house on ten acres. Close to Twin Cities. Fifty-six foot houseboat included for those long, lazy days on the lake. Terms and length of stay negotiable. Call Bud at Walleye Property Mgement: 555-8972

Rick Dalton had seen the ad in Friday's paper. He'd called the number right away and spoken with Bud Tank-hurst, who told him that the lake in question was Lake Travis, and that the house was "A slice of the past with all the modern conveniences." And that yes, the property was still available. The owner would be willing to show Rick the house and grounds and possibly discuss terms that Sunday, June 29, at two in the afternoon.

Rick and his son, Toby, left Minneapolis at a little after one on the appointed day. It seemed like no time at all before they were turning off the highway and onto the narrow, winding road that would take them to the farm-house.

The countryside was just as Rick had hoped it might be: serene and lovely. Maples and ash trees loomed thick all around, so they drove through a tunnel of vibrant green. Rick rolled down his window to get a whiff of the fresh, moist air and to listen in on the songs of the birds and the steady drone of cicadas.

According to Bud Tankhurst, there were over fifty miles of shoreline in the many branches and inlets of Lake Travis. Eighty percent of that shoreline was privately owned, which kept the tourists to a minimum and meant that even though the lake was near the Cities, they saw few other cars on the road.

"Beautiful, isn't it, son?" Rick asked, as if he actually might get an answer.

But of course there wasn't one. A quick glance at Toby, in the passenger seat, reminded him not to get his hopes up. The five-year-old sat staring straight ahead, his thin face a blank.

Rick resisted the urge to ask, "Toby, did you hear me?" He'd asked that question too many times in the past six months. Silence had always been the answer.

Rick checked the numbers on the mailboxes as they passed driveways that wound off into the trees, presumably on their way to lakefront houses like the one he sought.

"Almost there," he said, when the numbers neared the one Bud Tankhurst had given him. He tried to speak casually, to show no frustration with his son's unwillingness to communicate. Dr. Dawkins, Toby's psychiatrist, said that it was important to talk to Toby, to include him in conversations, whether Toby seemed to respond or not. Dr. Dawkins said that Toby did hear and understand, that he was improving steadily, and that with time and the right kind of attention he would be just fine. Sometimes Rick wasn't so sure of that. But he followed the doctor's orders anyway, as best he could.

Rick slowed the car when the mailbox with the address

he sought loomed up on the right. "Here we are," he said, as if the words mattered. He turned into the gravel drive, spotting a shingled roof through the thick branches of the trees.

Two hundred yards later, he pulled up in front of a two-story house with white clapboard siding on the bottom story and shingles on the dormers and touches of gingerbread trim at the eaves. Rose trees lined the white-pebbled walk to the front porch—a deep, inviting porch, furnished with white wicker armchairs and love seats. There was even a swing.

A good-size expanse of lawn surrounded the farmhouse. There were several lush trees planted in the lawn, their leaves fluttering in the slight breeze. Above, the sky was soft as a baby's blanket, and as innocently blue. Behind the house lay the lake, which glittered invitingly in the afternoon sun.

"It's perfect," Rick said to Toby.

And just as he said that, someone inside the house decided it was time for a little rock and roll. *Loud* rock and roll.

Rick couldn't help grinning. "So much for perfection." He recognized the song: "Piece of My Heart." It had been a favorite of a reclusive girl who roomed down the hall from him during his last year at college. The singer was Janis Joplin, a blues-rocker who had lived hard and died young and whose wild, rough life was there in every raw, impassioned note she sang.

Rick glanced at Toby, and found blue eyes just like his own watching him.

"Stay here. I'll see what's going on." Rick had to raise his voice a notch to compete with the tortured wails that came from the house.

Toby granted his father a tiny nod. Or at least Rick thought he nodded.

But whether Toby had nodded or not, Rick knew it would be safe to leave him alone for a few minutes. Toby was emotionally unresponsive, but very well behaved. He might not acknowledge Rick's instructions, but Toby always did what he was told.

From the house, competing with Janis's agonized moans, came what sounded like the howling of a dog.

What the hell was going on in there?

Rick cast his blank-faced son one last reassuring glance and then went to find out.

By the time he'd lifted a hand to ring the doorbell, the dog inside was yowling as loud and hard as Janis. And Rick thought he could hear another voice, human and female, wailing right along with Janis and the dog. Of course, when he rang the bell, he got no answer. No one inside there could possibly hear anything over all the racket.

Rick tried the door; it was unlocked. He pushed the door inward on a foyer that smelled of sunshine and beeswax. Without the door to muffle it, the screeching and howling swelled even louder.

Stepping inside, Rick moved toward the sound, which came from beyond a pair of open doors to his left. He halted between the doors, on the threshold of an old-fashioned front parlor.

He saw immediately that there was a stereo on the far wall, from which Janis's voice was blaring. On the sofa across the room sat a Saint Bernard, its massive head tipped back, its throat working enthusiastically to produce an earsplitting approximation of doggy harmony.

The dog wasn't the only one trying to keep up with Janis. Between the door where Rick stood and the sofa where the dog yowled, a shapely brunette dressed in a spangled forties cocktail dress and gaudy platform shoes wiggled and wailed. She wore a fringed lamp shade for a hat, and she was shrieking right along with Janis and the baying Saint Bernard. Rick leaned in the doorway, wondering with some amusement what she would do when she turned around and discovered him standing there.

It took a few moments to find out. The brunette was too involved in her performance to realize that she'd attracted an audience. But the dog noticed Rick right away. It lowered its huge head, gave a deep, soft woof, and got down from the couch. Tongue lolling, it circled the dancing, singing woman, then loped over to Rick and nuzzled his thigh with a large, wet nose. Rick granted the animal a quick scratch behind a giant-size ear.

The woman went right on singing her heart out. Rick watched the action. Though he had yet to see her face, she looked great from behind. Apparently the lamp shade obscured her view of the dog, because it took her a while to figure out that the animal was no longer sitting on the sofa, bellowing along with her. Readjusting her lamp shade, she shimmied around, no doubt wondering where the dog had gone. She froze in midscreech when she caught sight of Rick.

"Oh!" She whipped the shade off her head, her creamy skin flooding with agonized color. "How long have you been standing there?" She had to shout to be heard over the din Janis was making.

Rick did his best to stop grinning. "Long enough," he yelled back.

She made a pained face. "I was afraid you'd say that."

"I rang the bell, but—"

She waved a hand. "Never mind. I understand." She

trudged to the bare-bulbed floor lamp in the corner, where she spent a moment putting the shade back where it belonged. After that, she marched over and turned off the stereo.

She started apologizing as soon as the music stopped. "You must be my prospective tenant. Excuse us. We just... Well, Bernie begged me to play Janis, so I did. He loves that song."

"Bernie," Rick echoed. "That would be the dog?"

"Um-hm."

"The dog can talk?"

"Not exactly. But he always gets his point across. When he wants to hear Janis, he brings me the CD."

"A bright dog."

"Extremely."

Neither of them paid much attention as the dog in question wandered out the door, wagging his tail and panting. The woman swiped moist hair off her brow, drew her shoulders back and closed the distance between them, holding out her hand.

"I'm Natalie. Natalie Fortune."

Rick took her hand. It was soft, a little hot from all that dancing and singing—and a nice fit in his. She smelled of clean sweat and soap and flowers. He introduced himself. "Rick Dalton."

Still a little breathless, she put a hand against her chest. "And there's a little boy, right?"

"Right."

She looked down at their joined hands, and he realized that the handshaking was already done. He released her. She stepped back just a little and gazed up at him. She had the most gorgeous big brown eyes he'd ever seen. "I, um, understood that you were going to be here at two."

He glanced at his watch. "I guess I'm a few minutes early."

She smiled, still blushing a little. "And I let the time get away from me." Her smile changed then; it became tender. "Hello." She was looking beyond him.

Rick turned to see Toby hovering just inside the front door, his little mouth quirking shyly upward in response to Natalie Fortune's greeting, his small hand resting companionably in the ruff of the Saint Bernard, which stood at his side.

Rick was stunned. His son had actually smiled.

Her ridiculous platform shoes clumping with each step, Natalie tramped right around Rick and across the hardwood floor of the foyer to Toby, where she dropped into a crouch. The big dog took a hint from his mistress and plunked down on his hind quarters. Together, Natalie and Toby petted the dog.

"I see you've already met Bernie," she said.

Toby nodded.

"And I'm Natalie. What's your name?"

"Toby. His name's Toby," Rick supplied quickly.

Toby reached out shyly and touched one of the bangles on Natalie's dress. A silvery laugh escaped her. In a vamp's voice, she said, "You like? Come zeez way, my darlink." Taking Toby by the hand, she rose. The Saint Bernard trailed behind as she led the boy back into the parlor, circling around the bemused Rick for the second time.

At one end of the sofa lay a huge old steamer trunk, its lid flung back, various articles of clothing spilling out. Natalie led Toby right to it.

"This trunk was my grandma Kate's," she announced. "It belongs in the attic." She pantomimed wiping her brow. "Don't ask me how I managed to get it down here.

Boy, was it heavy!'' She groaned. ''And how I'll get it back up is another thing.'' She shrugged. ''I'll think of something. Later. But for right now, Bernie and I have been having fun. I found this fabulous dress in there.'' She looked down at her bangles and beads and then up long enough to grant Rick a wink. ''Not to mention these incredible shoes. And some of my grandpa Ben's things are in here, too.''

She knelt by the trunk. Toby stood to her left, and the Saint Bernard dropped to his haunches on her right. ''You see, Toby, this house was my grandma and grandpa's 'second honeymoon' house.'' She began pulling things from the trunk. ''When they'd been married a long, long time and two of their kids were pretty much grown, they bought this house across the lake from their big mansion.''

She pulled out a flowered scarf, a wide-brimmed pink hat and a black patent-leather clutch purse, all of which she set on the floor. ''Do you know why they bought it? I'll tell you. They bought it because they realized they'd grown apart over the years and they needed to find each other again. This house was the perfect place for that. It was simple and quiet and comfortable and they both fell in love with it. And they hoped that they might fall in love with each other again when they stayed here.''

She lowered her voice to a conspiratorial whisper. ''And do you know what?'' Toby was watching her, his small face rapt. ''They did find each other again. Nine months after they spent one beautiful week here, my grandma had another baby.''

Natalie began dressing the Saint Bernard in the things she'd pulled from the trunk. ''It's true.'' She slanted the wide-brimmed hat just so on the dog's head. ''After one short stay in this house, Grandma Kate had my aunt Rebecca, who is only a few years older than I am.'' Natalie tied the flowered scarf around the dog's neck and stuck the purse in his mouth. Then she clapped her hands in delight and declared, ''He looks great, don't you think?''

Toby actually nodded. The dog thumped his heavy tail.

Natalie looked up and caught Rick watching her. She flashed him a quick grin, then rose and advised Toby, ''Go ahead without me. Bernie loves to play dress-up.'' Bernie managed to bark in agreement without dropping the purse from his big, droopy jaws. ''I'm going to show your father the house.''

She moved out from behind the trunk. ''Ready for the tour?''

Captivated, Rick heard himself say, ''Sure.''

She marched past him in her silly, glittery shoes. He fell in step behind her, but couldn't resist one backward glance at his son, who was trying on a World War II army helmet and ducking to avoid Bernie's affectionate tongue.

Natalie led him to the foyer and up the stairs first, explaining that the house had been thoroughly modernized four years before, that the kitchen had been remodeled and a bath and a half added.

''Now all the windows are double-paned.'' She smiled over her shoulder at him. ''And you'll even have air-conditioning, for those hot summer days.''

Rick listened to her little sales pitch, but his mind was on what had happened in the parlor. As they reached the top of the landing, he couldn't help remarking, ''You have a way with kids.''

She shrugged her padded shoulders, and the beadwork on her dress glinted in the buttery sunlight that spilled in the window over the stairs. ''Kids and dogs. What can I say?''

"Next you'll be telling me you're a kindergarten teacher."

"First and second grade, actually. I teach at the school in town."

"Town?"

"You came out from the Cities, right?"

"Yeah."

"Well, if you keep going on the road you took to get here, you'll come to Travistown, around the far end of the lake. Population three hundred and forty. We have our own school, though a few grades always get combined, and we have a market, a hardware store and a couple of gift and clothing shops. And Walleye Property Management, of course."

"Right. Bud Tankhurst is one of the agents there."

"Bud Tankhurst is the *only* agent there. He owns it and he runs it. His wife, Latilla, does the books for him."

"I see." Her eyes really were the biggest, brownest eyes he'd ever seen. And her face was…familiar.

Her smooth brow furrowed. "Is Toby all right?"

Rick tensed. "What do you mean?" He knew he sounded defensive.

She leaned against the banister. "I mean, is something bothering him? He seems…too quiet. I don't think he said a word just now."

Rick looked away. He'd been in this woman's house for ten minutes, max. She was a stranger. But she didn't *feel* like a stranger. She drew him. And in ten minutes, she'd already accomplished the impossible: She'd made his little boy smile.

He met her eyes once more. "Both Toby's mother and his maternal grandmother died several months ago. A car accident. Toby was in the car when it happened."

Natalie made a small sound of distress.

"Toby hasn't spoken since the accident."

"Oh... I'm so sorry...."

"His mother and I were divorced. And I...hadn't seen Toby in a while. That's why I'm interested in this place. Toby's doctor says Toby's making progress, but that he would get better even faster if we had more time together, just the two of us. Time for Toby to learn for certain that he can trust me. And time for me to get to know him better. Does that make sense?"

Those big eyes were full of understanding. "Yes, it does. Perfect sense." She came away from the banister. "Let me show you the rest of the house."

He thought that he could stand here talking to her forever, but all he said was "Yes, that's a good idea."

She pushed the doors open on two small bedrooms and showed him the bath the rooms shared. "These will go with the rental."

He looked across the hall at two closed doors. She caught the direction of his gaze and explained, "That's my bedroom, a bath and a sitting room. There's a master bedroom and a study downstairs, so I was hoping that maybe we could just leave my private rooms out of the arrangement—if it's only going to be you and Toby."

"I see."

"I'd adjust the rent accordingly, of course."

"If I take the place, that would be okay with me. There are more rooms than we'll need, anyway."

She led him back downstairs, through the study and the big master bedroom, with its private bath. There was also a spacious kitchen, a pantry and laundry room with a half bath. Between the parlor and the kitchen was a formal dining room. And branching off from the kitchen was a breakfast area and a big, open family room, which Natalie referred to as the great room.

Once Rick had seen it all, they settled at the breakfast table to talk things over. Natalie said she'd hoped to find a renter who would take the house "as is," with all her furniture.

"That would be fine with me. But if we do this, I'd like to use the study for Toby's bedroom. Sometimes he has nightmares, and I want to be close by."

"I understand. I wouldn't mind at all if you brought down one of the beds from upstairs."

"Great."

She was grinning. "I think this just might work out." She braced her elbow on the table and propped her chin on her hand.

It hit him then. He remembered a spread he'd seen in some glossy magazine. A gorgeous redhead sitting at a table with her chin in her hand and an impudent grin on her lips. Her eyes had captured him as he thumbed the magazine: big and brown and soft. Just like the eyes of the woman across from him now.

The caption under the picture had read Fortune's Face: *Your face*. Then, now and always...

He couldn't stop himself from asking, "You said your grandmother was named Kate? Kate Fortune?"

She sighed. "The truth comes out."

"*The* Kate Fortune? Of Fortune Cosmetics?"

"Yes."

"You know, you look a little like—"

"Allison Fortune." She said the name of the world-famous model and spokesperson for Fortune Cosmetics with resignation. "She's my sister. Actually, she's married now. Her last name's Stone. Allie Stone."

She didn't look very eager to say more, and Rick wished he'd kept his mouth shut. He remembered reading how her grandmother, an expert pilot, had died tragically over a year ago. The plane Kate Fortune was flying had crashed in the jungles of the Amazon. The body, from what Rick recalled, had been burned beyond recognition.

"If you decided to take the house," Natalie said, a little stiffly, bringing them back to the topic at hand, "the groundskeepers from my family's estate, across the lake, will look after the property, so you won't have any worries there. And a woman will come in once a week to clean the place."

"Fine."

She looked down at her hands, which she'd folded on top of the table.

"What?" he asked.

She met his eyes again, and her white teeth worried her bottom lip.

"You look as if there's something you don't quite know how to say."

She chuckled. "You're right."

"Just say it."

"All right. There's one condition, if you did decide to take the house."

"I'm listening."

"You'd have to take care of Bernie while you're here."

He really hadn't been prepared for that one. "You want me to watch your dog for you?"

Her face was flushed again. "I know, it's crazy. But Bernie comes with the house."

"But why?"

She glanced away, then back. "This is Bernie's home."

He knew there had to be more to it than that, but she was obviously reluctant to tell him what. Rick considered her request, remembering the sight of his son standing in the doorway, with his hand on the dog's neck. And there were ten acres of property around the house; enough even for a dog that large.

While he thought it over, Natalie provided more detail about her plans. "I'm renting the house because I want to take a long vacation. I'm going on a cruise of the Mediterranean. I'll be leaving July twenty-eighth, to return at the very end of August so I can get ready before school starts. But if the time frame's wrong for you, I can stay across the lake, at the family estate I mentioned, either before or after I leave for my trip. My parents have split up and my father's living alone at the estate now. He'd be glad to have me." Her big eyes clouded a little, making him wonder whether there was some problem with her father.

The Fortunes were a very important family. And since Kate Fortune's death, it seemed to Rick, there'd been a lot of news in the papers about them. A missing heir had turned up, and Fortune Industries stock was down. In fact, Jacob Fortune, CEO of the Fortune companies, had made the front page of the *Star Tribune* only this morning. The article had not been flattering. Could that particular Fortune be Natalie's father? If so, it was no wonder she was worried about him.

Rick studied the woman across from him, thinking how uneasy he'd been about this whole "vacation" idea. He was a professional man, after all. He'd started out with nothing, and the whole focus of his life had been making something of himself. He'd never had much time for kids—and he didn't understand what made them tick. The painful truth was, he'd been scared to death that he would blow this experiment royally.

But fifteen minutes ago, he'd seen firsthand that his

little boy could be reached. Natalie Fortune had reached him—just by smiling and saying hello.

Now, she was watching Rick anxiously, no doubt worried by his extended silence. "Mr. Dalton?"

"Call me Rick. What?"

"Is there some problem?"

"No. No problem at all. This sounds just right for us. And I'd be glad to look after the dog. I need a couple of weeks to arrange a leave of absence from my job and tie up my affairs in the Cities. So I'd like to move in on July twelfth, and stay until August thirty-first. And don't move across the lake unless you want to. It's a big house, and you're welcome to stay right here until you leave on your trip."

The smile she gave him then took his breath away. "Whew. Relief. That's what I'm feeling now. Capital *R*. I thought for a moment there that you were going to say this wasn't what you were looking for."

"No, this is exactly what I'm looking for."

"Good. Because you and Toby are perfect. Bernie will be so happy you're the ones."

"*Bernie* will be happy?"

She rolled her eyes. "I really wasn't going to go into it."

"Into what?"

"You'll think it's odd."

"Tell me."

She shrugged her spangled shoulders. "All right. It's like this. Bernie was my grandma Kate's dog. When she left me the house in her will, she stipulated that Bernie always had to have a home here. Also, until I get married, the house always has to be occupied."

Rick understood then why she'd seemed so uncomfortable when she requested that he look after the dog.

He couldn't help asking, "What does your getting married have to do with anything?"

Around her neck she wore a thin gold chain with a single charm, a golden rosebud, hanging from it. Her fingers closed around the charm. "If my grandmother were still alive, you can be certain that I'd ask her."

Rick shook his head, marveling at the eccentricities of the very rich.

"So. Do we have a deal?" she asked.

"You haven't named a price."

She did.

"That sounds more than fair," he said.

She stood. "I'll get you an application, then. But it's just a formality. If you want the house from the twelfth of July until the end of August, it's yours."

"I want it."

She got him the papers, then returned to the parlor to join Toby and the dog while Rick filled in all the blanks on the application.

"Finished?"

He looked up to see her standing in the door to the hall, still dressed in her forties finery, with Toby on one side and the dog on the other.

He grinned. "All done."

"Then leave those boring papers right there and come on. I want you to see the *Lady Kate*."

They all trooped out to the sloping expanse of lawn behind the house and down to the lake. She took them out onto a wide dock and into the attached boathouse, where the houseboat, that had been mentioned in the ad was moored next to a much smaller open-bowed ski boat.

"This is the *Lady Kate*, one of my grandpa Ben's favorite toys," Natalie explained fondly, patting the hull of the larger boat. "Grandma Kate liked speed and adventure. She was an ace pilot. She even had a hydroplane dock put in at the estate across the lake. And just a few years ago, she bought herself a matching pair of jet skis. She was forever harassing the rest of us to buzz around the lake with her. But Grandpa Ben had a quieter side. He liked long days on the lake with his fishing pole. Sometimes he'd take me with him. And more than once, he took my whole family—my dad and mom, my brother and sisters and me. We'd all stay the night out on the water." She laughed her musical laugh. "It was no hardship, I can tell you. The *Lady Kate* has all the conveniences of home. She'll be at your disposal during the time you stay here." For a moment, those enormous eyes met his. And he couldn't help thinking that he'd like more than the houseboat to be at his disposal.

He wondered at himself. In the past few years, since the debacle that had been his relationship with Vanessa, he'd been wary of women. But from the moment he stepped into Natalie Fortune's parlor, his usual wariness had seemed to fade away.

The big dog bumped against his side. And Toby, who was holding Natalie's hand, turned for the door that would take them out onto the open dock. The adults and the dog followed where the silent little boy led them.

Outside, the water lapped softly against the pilings and the wind ruffled the surface of the water and far off over the lake somewhere Rick actually imagined he heard the wild, laughing cry of a loon.

He wanted to forget all about Minneapolis and the architectural firm where he'd been working like a demon for nearly a decade now. He wanted to forget his expensive house on its nice suburban street and just stay here. Leave it all behind and remain forever in the rambling farmhouse by the lake with the son who had smiled today and the big, friendly dog and the enchanting woman who sang along to Janis Joplin wearing a lampshade on her head.

But none of that was possible—not for two weeks, anyway.

He smiled at his son. "It's time to go."

Two

Natalie waved goodbye as her new tenants drove off. Bernie bumped against her side. She knelt and ruffled his neck fur.

"You love 'em, don't you, boy?"

Bernie swiped at her with his big, sloppy tongue, letting her know just how happy he was. Natalie laughed and ducked away from his canine kisses. She was every bit as pleased as her dog.

Not to mention relieved. Five prospective tenants had come by yesterday; none of them had worked out. But now she could relax. She'd found just the right people to look after the house and Bernie. The silent, sad-eyed little boy was adorable. And Rick Dalton seemed ready to treat her house and her dog as if they were his own.

He was also a hunk, with his lean good looks and his warm, exciting smile. And she would be living right here with him for two weeks....

Letting out a little grunt of self-disgust, Natalie rose from petting the dog. It was only in her silly, romantic fantasies that men like Rick Dalton wanted a woman like her. In real life, she was much too ordinary to hold their interest for long. And besides, he was taking the house for his son's sake. He'd have his hands full trying to get to know that little boy of his. The last thing he'd be looking for would be a summer romance.

And Natalie wasn't looking for romance, either—at

least not until she got on that cruise ship and met some-one exotic and different. Then maybe she'd go in for a shipboard dalliance. So what if she'd never been the "dallying" type. There was a first time for everything, after all.

"Come on, Bernie." She started up the walk. Halfway to the porch, she heard the phone ringing. She broke into a sprint and almost turned her ankle on the step, thanks to the platform shoes from Grandma Kate's trunk.

She made it to the foyer extension just before the answering machine picked up in the study—and then she wished she hadn't hurried.

"Natalie, what took you so long?" It was Joel Baines, whom Natalie had dated exclusively for five years, until a month ago, when Joel broke it off.

At first, after Joel told her it was over, Natalie had been crushed. She'd wandered around the house in a bathrobe, beset by crying jags, wondering what was the matter with her. But then she'd come to her senses and realized that Joel had done her a favor; she'd faced facts. Joel had been with her for two reasons: because it stroked his ego to have a Fortune on his arm, and because she'd made herself so incredibly convenient—always there when he needed her, always ready to do things his way. She didn't need a man like him in her life.

Unfortunately, for the past few days, Joel had been having second thoughts about his decision to end their relationship.

Natalie hadn't. "Joel, stop calling me."

"But, Natalie..."

"I mean it. Listen. Do. Not. Call. Me. Again."

"Natalie, I was a fool."

"Joel, you *betrayed* me." He had confessed that he'd

been unfaithful, just before he told her that he was through with her.

"I never should have told you about my little mistakes," Joel said. "I can see that now."

"Just leave me alone. Please."

"I love you, Natalie. There's a big fat hole in my life with you gone. If you'll just—"

"Goodbye, Joel." She hung up.

And, for a moment, she felt really good. Really, completely in charge of her life and affairs.

But only for a moment. Then, through the door she'd left open when she raced for the phone, she saw her mother's white Mercedes as it fishtailed into the turnaround by the front walk. Erica Fortune stomped on the brakes and brought the car to a skidding stop, spewing gravel in her wake.

With a sigh, Natalie went out to meet her.

Erica emerged from the car wearing a beautiful white linen suit that should have been a mass of wrinkles, but wasn't. On Erica Fortune, linen didn't dare wrinkle.

"Oh, Nat. Thank God you're here."

"What is it, Mother?"

Erica smoothed back her shining silvery-blond hair with a slim, perfectly manicured hand. The huge emerald ring that matched her eyes glittered in the sunlight. In her other hand she clutched a rolled newspaper. "Here. Look." She held out the paper.

Reluctantly Natalie took it and opened it up. It was that day's edition of the *Star Tribune*.

"Bottom right," her mother muttered.

Natalie turned the paper over. And there was her father's face. Bad Business at Fortune Industries, the headline read.

"I just...I need to talk," Erica said, giving Bernie,

who had been waiting patiently for her to notice him, an absentminded pat on the head. Then she let out a small moan. "Oh, Nat, I just don't know what's *happening* with him. Do you know what that article says?"

Natalie shook her head.

"It dredges up all the old dirt all over again, accusing your father openly of sabotaging his own company. There's a lot about the total insanity of his selling his personal stock to that awful, incomprehensible Monica Malone."

Like Erica and Natalie's sister, Allie, Monica Malone had once been a Fortune Cosmetics spokesmodel—the very first one, decades ago. And along with becoming Fortune's Face, the woman had become the reigning queen of the silver screen. No one in the family could stand her, but it seemed she was always in the background somewhere, stirring up trouble—and never more so than recently, since Grandma Kate's death. She'd been buying up stock in the company wherever she could find it. And when it came out six months before that Jake had turned his own shares over to her, no one had known what to make of it—and they still didn't, because Jake adamantly refused to give a single reason for what he had done.

"And that's not all that's in there," Erica continued. "There's speculation about the fires at the Fortune labs, a rundown on the threats against Allie, a description of the company break-ins, and if you turn the page you'll be treated to a chart that shows how far the company stock has fallen. Jake gets the blame for not dealing with anything right.

"Oh, what's happened to him?" Erica moaned. "I just... I still can't understand why he would *do* such a thing. He's always put his duty to the family and the company above everything else."

Natalie was scanning the article. She looked up. "I can't see anything new here. It's just more of the same old stuff."

Her mother sniffed. "Yes, and now even more people know all about it, since it's a front-page story in the Sunday edition."

Natalie asked carefully, "Mom, what can you do about this?"

"What do you mean?"

"I mean, are you going over to see Dad? Is that it?"

"No. I can't do that. You know I can't. Jake and I are hardly speaking."

"Well, then, maybe it's a mistake to get all worked up."

Erica shook her head. "I can't help myself. I've been furious with your father for a long time now. But lately, I... Nat, a woman can't just forget all about a man she's spent thirty years of her life with."

Natalie knew what was really bothering her mother: Erica still loved Jake. And Jake still loved *her*. Natalie wished they would work through their differences and reunite. But she was not going to get sucked into the family drama this time around. She had spent too many years playing confessor, comforter and caregiver to her family—as well as to the men in her life. And now she was bound and determined to make things different for herself.

"Nat..."

"What?"

"You know, if anyone could get through to your father, it would be you. You're so reasonable and level-headed, and you always know just what to say to get people to open up to you."

Natalie looked straight into her mother's gorgeous green eyes. "Mom, we *have* talked about this. I won't play go-between. Not anymore. And that's that."

Erica was quiet. Somewhere in the trees beside the house, a bird trilled out a few bars of song. Then Erica nodded. "Of course. You're right. I know you are."

In spite of her determination not to play the role of rescuer, Natalie ached for her mother. Within Erica there had always been a deep vein of dissatisfaction, of restlessness, though the world saw only a beautiful mask of cool ice-princess control. Lately, since Erica and Jake had separated, the veneer of cool control seemed to be cracking around the edges, while the fitful unhappiness was more and more obvious.

Natalie tucked the paper under one arm and put the other around her mother's proud, model-straight shoulders. "Come on inside. I have some iced tea already brewed."

Her mother perked up a little. "You're a lifesaver, Nat. If we could just sit and talk for a while, I know I'll feel better."

"And that's just what we'll do. Come on."

But Erica had stepped outside her own misery enough to notice what Natalie was wearing. She stood back. "What in the world have you been up to?"

"Dress-up." Natalie was glad for the chance to lighten the mood. She turned in a circle, vamping. "Do I look *fabulous,* or what?"

Erica groaned. "Or what."

Natalie shimmied her shoulders and shook her behind. "You're just jealous, that's all. You cool, understated types never get to wear the bangles and beads."

Erica tipped her blond head to the side. "You know, fifty years ago, it would have been showstopping."

"Fifty years ago, I'm sure it was."

"Where did you get it?"

"I found a trunk in the attic."

Erica laughed, then considered. "That dress was not Kate's. It's too flashy for Kate."

"I thought the same thing. But who knows? Whoever it belonged to, it was in the trunk, and I couldn't resist trying it on."

Both women grinned, then grew somber. And then, as so rarely happened now, Natalie was the child again, looking to her mother for comfort.

"I miss her, Mom."

And Erica was the one putting a consoling arm around her daughter. "We all do, honey."

Natalie leaned into her mother's embrace. "It's as if the world is spiraling out of control, since we lost her."

"I know. Oh, I know."

"I can't help feeling that if she were here, everything would be all right. She'd get right to the bottom of this...problem with Dad. And she'd take care of that awful Monica Malone. And she'd know right away if Tracey Ducet was the phony we all thinks she is." Tracey, who was the image of Natalie's aunt Lindsay, had recently surfaced claiming to be Lindsay's lost twin— and thus the heir to a huge chunk of Fortune assets. Sterling Foster, the Fortune family's longtime attorney, had been investigating her claim, privately saying it was false, but unable to prove anything, since the FBI records seemed to have been lost somehow.

"But Kate is not here," Erica said sadly. "And we must accept that."

Natalie leaned even closer to her mother. At the same

time, she felt for the chain around her own neck, and the rosebud charm at the end of it. The rosebud was a talisman from her grandmother; Kate had left a different charm to each of her children and grandchildren.

"Mom?"

"Hmm?"

"Sometimes I feel that she *is* here. Do you know what I mean? That she's watching over us. That she'll never let real harm come to any of us."

"Oh, Nat," Erica murmured tenderly, "you always were the most sentimental of all my babies."

"Okay, so it's corny. But still, it's how I feel."

Erica made a sound of understanding and stroked Natalie's hair.

Then Natalie stepped back. "Now come on." She took her mother's hand. "Let's go in. I could use a little iced tea myself."

Hand in hand, mother and daughter walked up the white-pebbled walk between the rose trees to the house.

Neither of them noticed that Bernie didn't follow. The big dog had wandered down to the boat dock behind the house.

And during the whole time Natalie and her mother were sharing iced tea and sympathy at the breakfast table, Bernie sat at the end of the dock, staring longingly out over the water to where a blue-and-white patio boat floated lazily on the slow currents of the lake.

"This is pure foolishness, Kate. And you know it." Sterling Foster rose from the pilot's chair of the patio boat and went to stand in the bright sun at the bow.

Kate watched him. He was a handsome man, tall and still trim, even in his mid-sixties, his shoulders straight and square. His hair was thick and white as snow. Kate had always liked him and admired him. In the past eighteen months, since the plane crash, she supposed it had gone beyond mere liking. But she stopped there. Her whole life was on hold until this crisis was solved. She had never planned to stay "dead" for this long, but she couldn't figure out how to come back without destroying all that she had accomplished—and all she had yet to do.

Kate's best friend wasn't pleased with her now, though. He turned and focused penetrating blue eyes on her. "You're a very distinctive-looking woman."

"Why, thank you, Sterling."

He glared at her. "Dark glasses and a big hat aren't going to hide you from someone who knows you."

Smiling a little, Kate glanced down at herself. She wore a teal-blue silk tunic and trousers to match, a wide straw hat tied with a scarf, and large dark glasses, which were intended to camouflage her face. "Don't be testy, Sterling."

He let out a low grunt of disgust. "I'm not testy. I'm realistic. You lived at the estate for years. Most of the people in Travistown knew you personally. Anyone floating by on another boat might recognize you."

Kate gave him a small shrug of her shoulders and looked away, out toward the farmhouse where, years and years ago, she and Ben had been happy. Her sweet, big-hearted Bernie was there, sitting so patiently on the end of the dock. The dog had been waiting in the same spot for nearly an hour now. Kate's heart went out to him. He would have to wait a while longer before he would see his old mistress again.

Kate wondered how Natalie was doing. Since her "death," more than one of Kate's loved ones had stumbled upon love and fulfillment. The truth was, Kate had been taking a secret pleasure in a little matchmaking—from beyond the grave, as it were.

And in the past few weeks, she'd been thinking of Natalie. A lot. Sterling, who kept her informed about all her children and grandchildren, had told her that Natalie and Joel Baines had broken up. Kate thought that was great news. She'd met Joel more than once, and she hadn't been impressed. Now maybe Natalie could begin looking for the real thing.

Sterling interrupted Kate's thoughts. "I will remind you, Kate, that you're the one who keeps insisting you can do more behind the scenes to discover who's trying to destroy the Fortune name and all it stands for than you ever could working in the spotlight. If you're recognized today—"

"I know, Sterling. I know. And you're right. It would be…unfortunate if I were recognized. But I won't be."

Sterling's response was a muttered expletive, and nothing more.

Kate softened her tone. "Sterling, please try to understand. I needed to come here today. So much of my life has been here…." She turned her head away from the farmhouse, toward the huge estate that she and Ben had built together in the first, heady years of their success. She couldn't see it from here, of course, but she knew it was out there, that it stood as proud and indomitable as ever, a huge, columned edifice of echoing, high-ceilinged rooms. At one time, in spite of all its opulent grandeur, it had been home.

Of course, when Kate thought of the estate these days, she thought of Jacob, too. Jacob lived there now. Alone.

"Kate?" Now Sterling was sounding almost gentle.

Kate shook herself. "Sorry. Just thinking."

Sterling's thoughts paralleled her own. "Jake *is* a

problem. If this stock situation isn't handled, he could lose everything you and Ben worked your lives to build."

Kate stopped him with a wave of her hand. "Not now. Please." She turned her head once more, so that she could see the farmhouse again. Her beloved Bernie was still there, waiting for her....

"What're you up to, boy? I've been looking all over for you."

The dog turned and whined a little, then looked at the lake once again.

Natalie shaded her eyes and stared out at the faraway patio boat that floated on the wind-ruffled surface of the water. It was one of the rentals.

"Sorry, big fella." She patted his flank. "It's no one we know. Come on, let's go inside. I want to change out of this dress and haul that trunk back up to the attic where it belongs." Natalie turned for the bank. But she only got a few steps before she realized the dog hadn't fallen in behind her. She slapped her thigh. "Come on."

With one last, longing look at the water, the dog did as she commanded.

"Look, Sterling," Kate said. "It's Natalie." Kate lifted the pair of binoculars she'd set on the seat. "Oh, my. She's been up in the attic, I see." Kate recognized the spangled dress and sparkly platform shoes. It had been long out-of-date when Kate herself wore it—for a Halloween costume at a party twenty years before.

The faraway figures of the woman and the dog turned and walked toward the farmhouse. "She needs love." Kate lowered the binoculars. "Real love, a man who'll give to her as she's always given to everyone else. That's why I left her the farmhouse. Ben and I found such joy there. Maybe she will, too. And Bernie will help. That dog has a nose for people. He never did care much for Joel Baines." She laughed. "Remember the first time Natalie brought Joel to the estate? Bernie chased him into the butler's pantry and kept him there for ten minutes, until the rest of us figured out what was going on and called Bernie off."

Kate could see that Sterling was trying not to smile. "I don't believe I remember that," he said.

"Oh, yes, you do. You were there for dinner that night. You tried not to laugh then, too, as I recall. But it doesn't matter. What matters is, Natalie is free of Joel now. Free to find a man who adores her and appreciates her and will spend his life showing her just how much."

Sterling put on a disapproving frown. "Don't you think maybe you're carrying this matchmaking thing a little too far, Kate?"

"No, I don't. Not at all. One can never take anything too far, if love is the prize."

Sterling looked doubtful. "But what was the point of the stipulation that the house has to remain occupied at all times until Natalie marries?"

Kate smoothed a wrinkle from her silk trousers. "Oh, I wasn't planning on dying for quite a while, and you know how I always fiddled with my bequests. At the time I thought it sounded right."

Sterling grunted. "Well, what you've done is made it all more complicated. Every time the poor woman wants to go somewhere, she has to find someone to stay at the house."

Kate chuckled. "She seems to be managing. And I want to know everything that's happening with her. Keep in close touch with her, won't you?"

"You know I always do."

* * *

The next day, Natalie was cutting roses to put in the parlor when Sterling Foster arrived in his big maroon Lincoln Town Car. Natalie ran out to meet him. In many ways, over the years, the family's longtime attorney had become like another member of the family. She greeted him with a hug and led him into the house.

"So, what are you up to lately?" he asked as she poured him a tall glass of lemonade.

She told him all about the details of the cruise. He already knew she was going, of course, since he was the one who managed her trust fund.

He listened to her plans and said he thought they sounded terrific. "But remember," he cautioned, "by the terms of your grandmother's will, this house must stay occupied and Bernie must be cared for here."

She reassured him that she hadn't forgotten, and explained all about the great tenants she'd found. "They're moving in on the twelfth, a while before I'm slated to leave. But it's all worked out perfectly, because Rick says it's fine with him if I stay right here until I'm ready to go."

"Rick?"

"Yes. Richard Dalton. His little boy is named Toby. Rick's an architect. With Langley, Bates and Shears, in Minneapolis."

"Did you have him fill out an application?"

"Of course." She grinned. "And I even read it over. That's how I found out he's an architect."

"Meaning you're not planning to check him out."

"I'm an intuitive kind of person, Sterling. You know that."

He gazed at her patiently. "May I have a look?"

"Oh, Sterling...."

"Be intuitive, Natalie. But let me check him out."

Natalie hesitated. She really did think Rick and Toby were just the tenants she'd been seeking. But then, she'd also thought that Joel Baines was the man she'd spend her life with.

"Oh, all right." She went to the study and came back with the papers Rick had filled out. "If you find out something bad, you'd better tell me right away."

"I will. I promise."

Three

The phone was ringing as Natalie staggered in from the small enclosed side porch that served as a mudroom in winter. She was lugging several bags from a number of exclusive Minneapolis boutiques. She dropped the bags inside the door and raced for the kitchen extension.

It was Sterling, calling to tell her that Rick Dalton had checked out just fine.

"It's about time you called me," she chided. "They're due to move in two days from now."

"Sorry. I wanted to do a thorough job."

"I'll bet."

"And there's no problem, anyway. I'm sure he'll make a fine tenant."

"I told you that over a week ago."

"I know, I know. Intuition wins again. But isn't it nice to know that the facts support your instincts?"

Natalie agreed that it was. Smiling, she thanked Sterling for looking out for her. Then, after promising to meet him for lunch before she left for the Mediterranean, she said goodbye.

She was turning to pay some more attention to her glamorous new wardrobe when the phone rang again. She picked it up.

And then immediately wished she hadn't.

"Natalie. I called just a minute ago. The line was busy."

"Joel. Give it up."

"Natalie, we have to talk."

"No, we don't. Goodbye, Joel."

He was still begging her to talk to him as she gently replaced the receiver. She looked over at Bernie, who had stretched out on the floor a few feet away, his head on his paws.

"Some people just don't understand the word *no*."

Bernie lifted his head and yawned hugely.

"My sentiments exactly." She started for the side door and her waiting bags of beautiful clothes, but then decided that maybe she ought to check her messages first. After all, she had been gone all day.

In the study where she kept the answering machine, she found there was only one message. From a soft-spoken woman with a British accent.

"Hello. My name is Jessica Holmes." On the tape, the woman paused, then sighed. "Oh, this is so difficult. Actually, I'm calling because I'm seeking relatives of a Benjamin Fortune. I thought perhaps... I don't know how to put this—except to say that the matter is extremely urgent. I would greatly appreciate a call back if you are related to, or know of, a Benjamin Fortune, aged in his seventies, who served in France during the Second World War." The voice left a London number and said goodbye.

Torn about what to do next, Natalie hovered by the machine as it squeaked and beeped and reset itself. As one of the few people in her family who kept a listed number, Natalie often paid the price for being so accessible; she got a lot of crank calls.

Total strangers had contacted her on more than one occasion with "urgent" messages. Inevitably they turned out to be reporters trying to get an inside scoop, or would-be wheeler-dealers who thought someone from the Fortune family might be interested in getting in on the ground floor of whatever money-making scheme they'd dreamed up.

No one before had mentioned Grandpa Ben, though. That was a slightly different angle.

Natalie replayed the woman's message and actually went so far as to start to dial the number Jessica Holmes had left. But then she shook her head and put down the phone. She was sure of what would happen: The woman would turn out to be working some kind of angle. And Natalie had dealt with people like that one time too many.

As the machine reset itself, she thought again of getting back to the job at hand: her new wardrobe. She'd spent three days in Chicago last week, buying everything in sight. And today she'd driven into the Cities to pick up a few other things. She was going to be *très* glamorous at the railing of that cruise ship, her hair blowing in the wind off the Strait of Gibraltar. Or maybe dancing on the tables in some picturesque Greek restaurant, drinking too much retsina and staying up until the crack of dawn.

But then it occurred to her that Rick Dalton and his little boy would be arriving in two days' time. And Rick wanted to put Toby here, in the study, so that he'd be nearby if Toby had bad dreams during the night.

It was definitely time to move some furniture around. And she'd need some help; her back had been sore for two days after she dragged that old steamer trunk back up to the attic. Natalie picked up the phone and dialed the number of the big house across the lake.

When the morning finally came that he and Toby returned to Lake Travis, Rick was more than ready to go. Though it was hotter and muggier than it had been that day two weeks before, the drive through the countryside was every bit as lovely as the first time. Rick simply kept the windows up and let the air-conditioning do its job.

As they neared the farmhouse, Rick was conscious of a rising feeling in his chest, a lightness, a sense of pure anticipation at the prospect of seeing Natalie Fortune again.

It was crazy, and he knew it, but he couldn't get the enchanting brunette out of his mind. He knew he'd thought about her way too much in the past weeks, about her big brown eyes and her shining coffee-colored hair and the subtle perfume she wore that seemed both floral and musky at once. And about the way Toby had responded to her and her huge, friendly dog. After that visit, Toby had seemed more withdrawn than ever by comparison.

Rick gave the boy a quick glance. Miracle of miracles, Toby met his gaze.

"Excited?" Rick asked.

He got no answer, but he was sure he saw Toby's little mouth quirk. Rick chose to take that as another positive sign that this vacation was going to be the best thing that had ever happened to either of them.

When they pulled into the turnaround in front of the walk, the captivating Natalie was there on the lawn, as Rick had secretly imagined she might be. She wore cutoffs and a snug T-shirt, and she was laughing, tossing a big stick for that lumbering, wonderful dog of hers to fetch.

Rick's heart did something impossible inside his chest. Dressed that way, with her hair caught back in a messy ponytail and sweat from the heat and the exercise making her skin gleam, she was Rick Dalton's living, breathing fantasy of the girl next door. No one would guess that she was actually a daughter of one of America's wealthiest and most famous families.

She gave them a wave and tossed the stick overhand. It sailed, end over end, through the air. The dog loped off after it, and she jogged over to the car. Rick rolled down his window.

She stopped a few inches from his door. "Right on time." She was panting. Sweat had darkened her shirt beneath her arms and between the soft swells of her breasts. Rick would have sworn he could smell her: flowers and musk. He felt a hard, thoroughly inappropriate kick of arousal, one that tightened his slacks and cut off his air.

He forced himself to breathe, grimly reminding himself that his son was sitting in the passenger seat beside him and he hardly knew this woman.

Right then, the Saint Bernard came bounding up, the stick Natalie had thrown for him clutched in his jowls. Natalie's quicksilver laugh rang out as the dog headed straight for Toby's side of the car. Once he reached the passenger door, the huge animal sat, dropped the stick and gave a low, friendly woof.

Toby flung open his car door, jumped down and wrapped his too-thin arms around the dog. Rick watched, his heart aching in his chest.

He glanced at Natalie. She met his eyes and smiled— a soft, quivery-lipped kind of smile. She understood what a step Toby had just taken. And she was moved.

A moment ago, Rick had wanted her desperately. Now he just plain adored her. There wasn't a doubt in his mind now that the woman and her dog were absolute magic.

When he looked back at his son, Toby was already lugging the big stick out to the lawn. Bernie trotted along behind him.

"Come on," Natalie said. "Let's get your things inside."

Rick popped the trunk latch from inside the glove compartment. When he got out and went around to the back, Natalie was there ahead of him, pulling two bags of the groceries he'd bought into her capable arms. He hauled out a couple of suitcases and followed her up the walk, pausing to call a reminder to Toby that he wasn't to wander off anywhere. Toby turned and looked at him, which Rick knew meant the boy had heard and understood.

Inside, Rick found that Natalie had already made the study over into a bedroom. He set Toby's suitcases down and admired the changes while Natalie went on out to the kitchen to drop off the grocery bags. Rick was still surveying the room where his son would sleep when she appeared in the doorway.

"I had a couple of my father's men come across the lake to help me out," she explained. "We switched the furniture in here with the stuff from the room at the top of the stairs."

Rick was standing on the far side of the bed. He touched the bedspread, which was quilted and stenciled with airplanes. "I don't remember seeing this upstairs."

Her cheeks flushed an adorable shade of pink. "All right. I confess. I bought the bedspread just for Toby." She moved into the room, across the bed from him, and touched the wooden propeller of the airplane lamp that sat on the nightstand. "And I bought this lamp." She pointed at the airplane mobile in the center of the room. "And that, too. I thought Toby would like them."

They looked at each other across the airplane quilt. Rick spoke around the sudden lump in his throat. "It was kind of you. To go to the trouble to fix up the room for him."

"No trouble. Really."

"You'll let me reimburse you."

"No, I won't."

He started to protest.

She put a finger to her lips. "Shh. Not another word about it." She turned for the door. "Now, come on. We haven't finished unloading the car yet." And she was gone, leaving him no choice but to follow. Which he did, after a moment spent grinning like a idiot at the airplane mobile rotating slowly in the slight breeze created by the air-conditioning vents.

Within half an hour, Rick had all of his and Toby's things put away and his car parked next to Natalie's in the big garage on the south side of the house.

Natalie was showing him where to put his groceries when he told her he wanted to take the *Lady Kate* out onto the lake for a picnic lunch.

"That okay?" he asked.

"Of course. Sounds like fun."

Rick picked up the last bag, which was full of packaged goods, and headed for the laundry room and the small pantry closet there.

Natalie watched him go, reminding herself, as she'd been doing ever since the man and the boy arrived, that Rick was the tenant and she was the landlady. And that was all.

The problem was, Rick seemed even more attractive now than he had two weeks ago. His eyes seemed bluer, his shoulders broader. And every time he smiled at her, her stomach did the strangest things.

Her thoughts on Rick and not much else, Natalie went to the refrigerator and took out a package of deli-sliced ham, some spicy mustard and a big jar of kosher-style dills.

"What are you doing?" Rick asked. He was standing in the short hall from the laundry room.

She froze and looked down at the food in her hands.

And it came to her: She'd been about to make him some sandwiches. She was the landlady and he was the tenant and nothing in the rental agreement said a thing about meals. And yet he'd mentioned the word *lunch* and she'd automatically started making it.

She was just a hopeless case—that was all there was to it. Get her near an available man, and the first thing she did was start fixing his food for him. It had been that way with Joel. She'd loaned him money when he was short—some of which he never had paid back. She'd graded his papers and cleaned his little cottage in town. She'd bought his groceries when she bought her own— and then been waiting for him every night when he showed up at her door with his dirty laundry under his arm and "What's for dinner?" on his lips.

Rick clearly had no clue of the direction of her thoughts. He was grinning. "Lunch is already made. I stopped at a deli before I left Minneapolis."

"Oh, really?"

"Yeah. They even put it in a nice big picnic basket. It's got everything—including paper plates and plastic forks. I left the basket on the front porch. Maybe you didn't see it."

She sincerely prayed that her face wasn't as red as it felt. "Um. No, I guess I didn't." Very carefully, she set the sliced ham back in the meat drawer and the mustard and pickles on a shelf and closed the refrigerator door. "Listen. I've got a few things to do. I should probably just get busy on them."

He folded his arms and leaned against the little section of counter that projected off the wall to the laundry room. "Damn. I was hoping you'd come with us."

Her heart lifted. It was ridiculous. She had to get a grip on herself here. "You were?"

"Yeah." He was wearing a dark blue knit shirt and khakis. The shirt clung to the hard contours of his shoulders. And with his arms folded like that, the muscles of his biceps were starkly defined. And his dark hair was so shiny, it even curled a little. It was the kind of hair any woman would want to run her fingers through. And he had the nicest mouth. It was firm, but there was fullness to it. Natalie thought that it would probably be a wonderful mouth for kissing—a mouth that could command and beguile at the same time.

"Natalie."

"Um. Yes?"

"Come with us."

"Oh, I really shouldn't. You know how it is, when you have so many things to—"

"Please?"

And her own mouth just opened and she heard herself say, "Okay."

He stopped leaning on the counter. "Great." He looked so cool and collected.

And she realized that she felt sticky and grungy in her old cutoffs and sweaty T-shirt. "Listen. Could you give me a few minutes? To clean up a little."

"Take all the time you need." He started walking toward her.

She backed away, all nerves and confusion. She shouldn't be going with him. She shouldn't have said yes. He was renting her house for a couple of months, she reminded herself for what had to be the hundredth time.

And that was all that was supposed to be going on here. "A few minutes. Really. I won't be long."

He stopped in the middle of the kitchen. "I'll go out and hunt down Toby and the dog."

"Yes. Do that. Good idea." She backed around the central island that contained the stove, and then just kept walking backward toward the main hall. Rick watched her go.

As soon as she lost sight of him, she realized how silly she must look, walking backward through the hall. So she turned around, squared her shoulders and marched, head high, up the stairs.

She came down twenty minutes later, freshly showered and dressed in white shorts, a red silk camp shirt and a pair of sandals. The shower and the change of clothes had helped a lot. She felt much more in control of herself—until Rick smiled at her and told her she looked great and she felt like a tongue-tied teenager all over again.

They all trooped down to the dock out back and into the boathouse where Rick put the lunch basket in the big galley of the cabin, and then got a quick lesson in how to operate the boat from Natalie. Since no one planned to water-ski, they left the smaller boat behind.

For their first time out, Natalie backed the *Lady Kate* from the slip inside the boathouse, so that Rick could see how it was done. Then, once they were launched and pointed in the right direction, she turned the wheel over to Rick.

Several miles out, they turned off the big engine and let the boat drift. Rick brought out the lunch. More than once as they devoured the lemon roast chicken and pasta salad, Rick teased Toby that Bernie would get fat if he didn't stop slipping him treats.

"And look how big he is already," Natalie said. "If he gets fat, he'll fall through the floor of the farmhouse."

"He'll sink the boat," Rick warned.

Natalie couldn't resist adding, "The dock will collapse when he wanders out onto it."

Toby just looked at them—and gave Bernie the last hunk of his dinner roll.

When they'd eaten their fill, the child and the dog stretched out on the deck, while Natalie and Rick made themselves comfortable on the padded benches that lined the bow. They leaned on the railing and gazed off at the shoreline, picking out the houses that could be seen here and there between the trees.

"There. Look. That's my family's estate." Natalie pointed at a huge green expanse of lawn on a faraway bank. The lawn swept up to a graceful stone balustrade and a wide terrace. Behind the terrace loomed an imposing Greek Revival-style house, its many windows glittering like jewels in the afternoon sun.

"Impressive," Rick said.

A wave of sadness washed over Natalie. Once, the huge house had been like a second home to her. But now, with her father living there alone save for the small army of staff the place required, it just wasn't the same. She'd spoken to her father two days before, when she'd asked him to send help to switch the furniture around for Toby. He'd sounded awful—distracted and distant. In spite of her determination to steer clear of family turmoil, she hadn't been able to stop herself asking him if he was all right.

He'd laughed; it had been a grim, depressing sound. And he'd told her not to believe everything she read in the papers, that he was getting by.

Now, she found herself telling Rick, "When I was a

little girl, it seemed as if we used to spend more time in that house over there than at our own house in Minneapolis. We'd come out on weekends, even in the deepest heart of winter, when the grounds were covered in a blanket of white and we had to spend most of the time indoors. And in the summer, we'd sometimes come and stay for weeks at a time. Grandma Kate and Grandpa Ben lived there together, right up until he died, about ten years ago. When I was little, my aunt Rebecca— She's Grandma Kate and Grandpa Ben's youngest. Maybe you've heard of her?''

"Rebecca Fortune...the mystery writer?''

"That's the one. Anyway, Aunt Rebecca was still a child, too. So she lived at the estate. And my uncle Nathaniel used to bring his family for visits, the same as my dad and mom brought us—all the time. So the place always seemed like it was full of kids. Overflowing with activity. Laughter and happy shouts just bounced off the walls.''

Rick was watching her, smiling a little. "How many brothers and sisters do you have?''

"Three sisters, one brother.''

"A big family.''

"You actually sound jealous.''

"I am,'' he admitted. "I was an *only*.''

"You wanted siblings?''

"You bet I did.''

She couldn't resist confessing, "There have been times I would have gladly given away one or two of mine.''

"Which ones?''

"Is that a fair question?''

"Natalie. Come on.''

"Oh, all right. The twins. Allie and Rocky.''

"Allie's the model.''

"Yep. And Rocky looks just like her. They're identical. Two of the most gorgeous women in the world—even though Rocky never went in for the glamour route. She's a pilot, like Grandma Kate."

"Why would you have given them away?"

"Did I say that?"

"Come on. Spill it."

She laughed. "All right. Because I was so jealous of them, that's why. They always had each other, no matter what else went wrong. They had that *thing* that identicals so often have. A world of their own. It was sometimes as if they could read each other's minds, you know? And even though they were two years younger than me, which should have given me some kind of edge over them, I was the one who felt left out."

"So you were jealous of their closeness."

"Yes. And that's not all."

"I'm listening."

And he was. Listening. So intently. As if he really cared. She felt her cheeks coloring. "Why am I telling you all of this?"

"Because I asked. Go on."

"It's not important."

"Natalie." He looked at her levelly. "I want to hear it."

She believed him. She shouldn't, she knew it. But she did. She heard herself confessing, "Well, to me it always seemed that, between the two of them, Allie and Rocky were perfect."

"Perfect?"

"Um-hm. They seemed to have every single desirable trait that I lacked. Beauty and courage, a spirit of adventure, an air of excitement that followed them both wherever they went. And you know what?"

"Uh-uh."

"They're both still like that. Gorgeous and brainy and brave and exciting." She rested a hand on the bench cushion and leaned toward him. "And Caroline, my older sister, is no slouch, either. The truth is, I'm the *boring* sister."

He faked a groan. "Are you fishing for compliments?"

She thought about that, then confessed, "Sure sounds like it, doesn't it?"

He leaned toward her, so there were only inches between their noses. She caught a hint of his after-shave, a fresh, outdoorsy scent, and found herself thinking that he smelled every bit as good as he looked.

He said, "You are not boring."

She sighed. Rick was a terrific guy.

Too terrific, a voice way back in her mind warned, *to ever want or need someone like you.*

She had to get some distance. Fast.

She shifted back away from him. "We should either drop the anchor or start up the engine again. We're getting a little too close to shore."

They started the engine. Toby, who'd been sitting on the deck with Bernie, got up and stood proudly beside his father as Rick took the wheel. At a cove Natalie knew, they dropped the anchor.

When she and Rick were settled on the padded bench once again, Natalie found herself asking him, "Are your parents still alive?"

Rick shook his head. "They died when I was in my teens. An electrical short that started a house fire. Late at night, while we were asleep. I woke up and managed to get Mom out, but couldn't find Dad. A neighbor saved me, but they... neither of them made it." He looked out over the water.

Not stopping to consider whether such a move was wise, she laid her hand on his. "How sad for you."

He looked down at where she touched him. "It was a long time ago. I went to live with my aunt and uncle, but they didn't have kids, either. Anyway, I always wanted a bunch of brothers and sisters. But you know what they say, if wishes were horses..." As his voice trailed off, he looked up into her eyes. Then, slowly, he turned his hand and wrapped his fingers around hers.

Natalie was stunned. It seemed at that moment like the most intimate thing any man had ever done to her—to turn his hand and take hers and look right into her eyes as he did it. Suddenly, the day seemed terribly hot, the air unbearably close and humid against her skin. And the hand that held hers was so warm and encompassing, sending little shivers zinging through her.

She realized he was smiling at something behind her. "What?" she asked, turning.

Bernie was stretched out on the deck, asleep. And Toby had used the dog as a giant-size pillow. The big brown-and-white belly cradled the small, dark head. The boy's eyes were closed, and his thin chest rose and fell in an even, shallow rhythm.

Natalie turned back to Rick again. He smiled at her, deep into her eyes. And for a moment, what they were doing—sitting here, holding hands as the boy and the dog slept so peacefully a few feet away—seemed the most natural, *right,* thing in the world to be doing.

But then reason reasserted itself.

Natalie Fortune, are you out of your mind? that voice in her head warned. *Before you know it, you'll be doing his laundry and raising that darling little boy for him.*

It occurred to her that there were worse fates.

And that was when she knew she was *really* in trouble

here. She'd barely gotten rid of Joel. In fact, Joel still refused to admit he'd *been* gotten rid of. It was way too soon to be falling for another man—and especially not a man like this. A man who was just too good to be true.

She pulled her hand free. He let it go.

There was an awkward, awful moment when she had no idea what to do next.

She glanced frantically out toward the water again, spotting a blue-and-white patio boat far off to starboard, past the mouth of the cove where they lay at anchor, and focusing on it to keep from looking at Rick. She squinted. The boat seemed to have two people aboard. She wished she was on it.

Anywhere but here, where she was having much too lovely a time for her own good—and where she kept doing and saying things she shouldn't.

"Natalie?" His voice was so gentle.

"Umm?"

"Are you…all right?"

"Of course," she lied.

She still didn't have the nerve to look right at him, so she went on staring at the faraway boat, her entire body tingling with a thoroughly dangerous kind of awareness. And though she still couldn't meet Rick's eyes, she knew very well that they were trained on her face.

And it *was* hot. She shifted around again, because the backs of her legs were damp from the leather seat pad. And she raised her arms and lifted her hair off her neck. The air caressed her damp skin, cooling it a little.

Rick was leaning on the railing.

She dared to give him what she hoped was a very casual kind of smile. "It's hot."

He went on watching her. "Very."

"Funny. When people think of Minnesota, they think of snow. But we have our summers, too."

"We certainly do."

She reached into the pocket of her shorts and found an elastic hair band, which she used to quickly tie her damp hair into a high ponytail. Then she straightened her shirt, which had pulled out a little when she lifted her arms. "Better," she said, and forced herself to smile directly at him.

It was a mistake. In his eyes there was a look—a questioning, hopeful look. And though her mind kept saying, "No" to that look, the rest of her was shouting, "Yes!"

She should say something totally innocuous now, she knew it. But she couldn't think of what.

So that meant he was the next to speak, and what he said wasn't innocuous at all. "I've been...alone for a long time now."

And then, with one or two glances at his sleeping son, he quietly began to tell her about his ex-wife, Vanessa Chandler, whom he'd met at a friend's Christmas party and married a year later. He frankly confessed that he hadn't put as much time and attention into the marriage as he should. He'd put so much energy into succeeding at work, there wasn't a lot left over for his marriage. Vanessa had felt neglected.

And then, later, he hadn't been much of a father to Toby. Vanessa had divorced him when Toby was only a year old, then moved back to Louisville, where her widowed mother lived, taking Toby with her. Visits with Toby had been few and far between. Vanessa would have been perfectly happy never to set eyes on Rick again, as long as he sent the support checks on time. And Rick had been so busy getting ahead that he didn't pursue his parental responsibilities as he should.

"So now," he said ruefully, "I'm trying to make it up to my son for all the times I wasn't there for him."

"I think you're making a pretty good start."

He muttered a thank-you, then asked, "What about you?"

"Was I ever married, you mean?"

"Yeah, for starters."

She shook her head. "Never married."

"What about 'meaningful relationships'?"

And then, there she was, telling him about Joel, how she'd met him when she first started at Travistown School and how they'd been together for five years. That Joel had called it off between them about a month before. That she had been deeply hurt at first, but had gotten past that.

"And now, I'm planning to fully enjoy my freedom."

"Hence the decadent extended cruise?"

"You got it. The cruise is my attempt to do something purely self-indulgent for once, something that has nothing to do with kids or dogs or other people's emotional needs."

Rick listened and nodded and seemed honestly interested in every word she had to say—which was probably why neither of them paid much attention when Toby rolled himself into a ball on the deck and stopped using Bernie for a pillow.

After that, Bernie sat and stretched and padded over to starboard, where he hefted his front paws onto the padded bench and stared at the patio boat that still drifted on the slow currents several hundred yards away.

Four

"The first time was chancy, Kate," Sterling said. "But this time is pure folly. And would you *please* put down those binoculars? We're close enough that the sunlight could reflect off the lenses and tip them off about what you're up to."

Kate pointed at the canopy overhead. "I'm in the shade." She adjusted the focus on the binoculars. She could see Bernie, looking back at her. And when she scanned to the right just a little, she could see the back of Rick Dalton's head and Natalie's sweet, gentle face. They were leaning close to each other, apparently deep in conversation.

"Kate." Sterling reached out and snared the binoculars from her hands.

She glared at him. "Sterling, really."

In two long strides he was at the stern, stowing the binoculars in the built-in chest there. "That takes care of that," he said, with way too much satisfaction, as he returned to sit beside Kate.

"Oh, all right. Have it your way." Kate retied the scarf she wore and adjusted her dark glasses. Then she produced a snowy handkerchief and blotted her brow. "It's much too hot to argue with you, anyway."

"You shouldn't be here."

"I know, I know." She patted his hand. "But I couldn't resist. I had to see the man and the boy for myself, that's all. And now I have. And I feel wonderful about them. They're going to be much more than just perfect tenants. Wait and see.''

Sterling grunted. ''Fine. Let nature take its course with them, then. We have some much more serious problems to deal with than whether Natalie will find herself a new boyfriend or not.''

''Nothing's more serious than love.''

''Do you know how low the company stock has fallen? Yesterday it closed at—''

''I know where it closed yesterday.''

''The shareholders are screaming. And every employee you've got is terrified about what will happen next. Security has been breached. Badly. The Secret Youth Formula...''

Kate waved her hand and Sterling fell silent. ''I know, I know.''

The Secret Youth Formula was Kate's pet project at Fortune Cosmetics, an as-yet-unperfected gel blended of certain herbs and vitamin extracts that could actually reverse the aging process.

Not too long ago, someone had broken into the lab and stolen the formula. Probably the same person who had set the series of fires at the labs. And tried to kill Kate. And sent a henchman to pretend to be a crazed fan who kidnapped Allie. And continued to make trouble.

''As of now, though,'' Kate reminded her friend, ''while it may not be business as usual, we are holding together.''

''Barely. Everyone's near the breaking point. Your two sons are at each other's throats. Nathaniel's always felt he could run the company better than Jake. And lately, with what Jake's been doing, I'm beginning to agree with him.''

"We'll get to the bottom of all of it. Eventually."

"But will we do it in time? On top of everything else, there's that damned Ducet woman."

"She's a problem, I know."

"She's more than a problem. She's a bad-press machine. She keeps giving interviews to the tabloids about how the family isn't accepting her."

"Since she is not my daughter, I don't see any reason why the family *should* accept her." Kate's lost child, the twin to her first daughter, Lindsay, had been a boy. Kate knew this. And so had Ben. But when the child was kidnapped, shortly after his birth, the FBI had ordered the information kept under wraps in order to maintain closer control of their investigation. The sex of the child had never been released to the public. And Kate, hurting too much to talk about it, had forbidden mention of the child over the intervening years.

Now, because of the lost FBI records, except for the kidnappers themselves, Kate was the only one whose statement could get rid of the fake heiress for good and all.

"The last thing we need right now is more bad press," Sterling said.

But Kate was firm. "I want Ms. Tracey Ducet to play her whole hand before we discredit her. I want to know what she's up to. And I want to find out if she's got anything to do with our problems—from the fires at the lab to the hijacker who caused my plane to crash."

"I'm not a nervous man, Kate. But I'm becoming very nervous lately."

"Just a bit longer, Sterling. I really must know who's behind all the terrible things that have been happening."

"I'm worried about Jake. Really worried. He behaves like a man about to do something desperate."

"Go see him. Right away. Try to get him to open up to you."

"Jake is your son. You, of all people should know the likelihood of his opening up to *anyone*, ever."

"Do what you can. And give me a full report." She stood and went to the stern.

"Kate. Don't..."

But she already had the binoculars out of the chest.

"Sometimes you're so damn reckless," Sterling muttered.

Kate only smiled and turned the focus on the binoculars, so that she could see the man and woman on the other boat.

On the *Lady Kate*, the conversation had drifted away. Natalie and Rick sat close together, both enjoying the silence. Natalie sighed and gazed over the railing. Even here, where it was shallow enough to drop anchor, the waters below the bow looked deep and still.

"What are you looking at?" Rick asked.

"It's not what I'm looking *at*. It's what I'm looking *for*."

He leaned over the side, close enough that their knees brushed, and looked into the water with her. "All right, Ms. Fortune. What are you looking *for*?"

She told him, in a teasing whisper. "The friendly monster of Lake Travis."

"The what?"

Still staring into the slightly mossy depths, she explained, "When I was a little girl, and Grandpa Ben used to take me out on this boat, he'd look over the edge into the water and say he saw a friendly monster down there."

Rick chuckled.

She looked up from the water and into his eyes.

They shared a smile.

Rick's glance strayed to her mouth.

Natalie knew then that he was going to kiss her. And she wanted him to kiss her. She knew it would be lovely. And warm. And tender. And arousing...

Not to mention a major error in judgment, some wiser voice far back in her mind chided her knowingly.

She froze, then straightened, pulling away from him.

Rick frowned. "Look, Natalie, I—"

Before he could say another word, she put up a hand. "We should get back."

He watched her for a moment, then nodded. "All right." He turned toward the deck.

They realized simultaneously that Toby and the dog were gone.

Rick stood, his thoughts all for his son now. "He never wanders off."

Natalie got to her feet, as well. "I'm sure they've just gone inside."

Rick was already at the cabin door.

Inside, they found Bernie sitting in front of a storage cabinet opposite the kitchen counter area. The dog looked at them, whined softly, then lifted a giant paw to scratch at the door of the cabinet.

Rick knelt and pulled open the door.

Toby was there in the dark space, his legs drawn up to his narrow chest and his arms wrapped tightly around his knees.

"Toby, come on out."

The boy huddled closer into himself and hid his head against his knees.

"Come on, now...."

Toby hunched up tighter still.

Natalie was standing behind Rick. When he looked around at her, she read the frustration in his eyes.

"He does this sometimes," Rick said. "Finds himself a tiny space and then won't come out of it. He used to do it a lot, but it's tapered off recently." He shook his head. "His doctor says I shouldn't make a big deal of it."

Natalie had an idea. "Why don't you join him?"

"What?"

"Just get in there with him."

Rick looked at her as if she were a few cards short of a full deck.

"Trust me. I'm right about this." She folded her arms and tried to look supremely confident, though she really had no way to be sure whether her idea would work or not. But in her experience, troubled children sometimes responded positively to adults who were willing to venture into their world with them. "Go on, Rick. Do it."

For several seconds, Rick didn't budge. But then, with a grimace, he dropped to his knees.

He cast her a glance that clearly said, *This had better work.* Then he instructed lightly, "Scoot over, son. Let me in."

Still hunched into himself, the boy slid deeper into the cabinet. Rick couldn't actually fit in there, but he did manage to stick his head and shoulders inside with his son.

Looking down at the long, khaki-clad legs that stuck out into the galley, Natalie suggested airily, "You two just enjoy yourselves. I'll power up the *Lady Kate* and get us back home."

From his cramped quarters in the cabinet, Rick heard the woman and the dog leave the cabin. A few minutes later, he heard the anchor being drawn up, and then the engine began to rumble.

Rick crossed his arms tightly over his chest—the only place they would fit—and tried not to crush the small body that was pressed against the inner wall of the cabinet.

"Do you feel safe in here, Toby?" he dared to whisper, though he knew there would be no answer.

Dr. Dawkins had told him not to be too concerned when Toby chose to hide, that confined spaces sometimes equalled safety to a troubled child. Every time it happened, Rick reminded himself of the doctor's words—and then felt worried as hell anyway. This time was no different from the others—except that now, having joined his son in the tiny space, he also felt like a damn fool.

But Natalie had suggested this. And Natalie seemed to have a sixth sense about Toby.

With a sigh, Rick settled in to endure the ride back to shore. Halfway there, Rick felt the touch of small fingers in his hair. It took him a moment to realize that his son was trying to take his head in his little hands. Rick did his best to move where Toby pushed him.

A moment later, his head was cradled on a pair of skinny knees. Rick put a lot of effort into keeping his weight off his son's fragile legs, and that gave him a stitch in his neck. But he didn't care. Not one damn bit.

When the boat finally came to a stop, Toby grunted and gave Rick's shoulder a shove. Rick twisted his way out of the cabinet and then scooted aside. Toby crawled right out behind him, with no need for coaxing at all. Of course, his small face was impassive. But so what? For a few moments, in the darkness of that cabinet, Toby had dared to reach out.

"Everything okay?" It was Natalie, standing in the door to the deck.

"Everything's terrific," Rick answered.

The sky had clouded over during the return trip to shore. As they docked the boat and carried the picnic basket back to the house, the first few drops of rain were falling. Rick tipped his head up to the rain and thought again that Natalie Fortune really was magic. And he was damn glad she'd be hanging around for the next two weeks.

And hell, he might as well be honest with himself. He was interested in her. Really interested. He wanted to get closer to her.

That surprised him. He'd been telling himself for four years now that he wouldn't be taking a chance with a woman for a long time to come. There had been too much bitterness in him, after Vanessa. But Natalie was *not* Vanessa. In fact, Natalie was unlike any woman he'd ever met. He wanted to know her a hell of a lot better.

True, she'd pulled away from his kiss out on the water. But he'd been pushing it a little fast, he realized now. He'd take his time, approach her more slowly.

After all, time *was* on his side.

Who could say what might happen in two weeks of being together, day in and day out?

Five

But just as Rick was consciously deciding that he wanted to get closer, Natalie was determining that a certain distance was going to have to be kept. As soon as she was safely in her own upstairs rooms, Natalie called her aunt Lindsay.

Lindsay Fortune Todd was a doctor who lived on the other side of the lake with her husband and two children. Their big, comfortable house wasn't too far from the family estate. Aunt Lindsay worked long hours at Minneapolis General Hospital as a staff pediatrician. Usually when Natalie called on the spur of the moment, her aunt turned out to be at work. But today she got lucky. Lindsay answered the phone.

"Nat," Lindsay said with great fondness. "Where have you been lately?"

Natalie pushed aside her guilt. Since she'd decided to change her life, she'd been avoiding situations involving the family. But right now, all the troubles in the family seemed like nothing to worry about when compared with the tender look in a certain pair of blue eyes.

"Why don't you come on over?" Lindsay asked. "Frank's barbecuing burgers tonight. If the rain clears off, we'll eat out on the deck."

It was exactly what Natalie had hoped her aunt would say. "I'd love to. I'll be there in an hour or so."

"My aunt Lindsay invited me for dinner," she told

Rick a few minutes later. He was sitting in the great room, thumbing through a magazine while Toby watched television, with Bernie at his side.

"Have a good time." He smiled at her, and her silly heart gave a sweet, scary lurch inside her chest.

He didn't seem the least upset about her going, and yet she felt like a rat for leaving him. All the more reason, she told herself, that she had to be very careful around him.

The rain stopped and the sky began to clear as Natalie drove around the lake to her aunt's house. When she pulled up in the drive, she noticed a sports car she'd never seen before parked by the front walk.

Wondering who'd stopped by, Natalie strolled up the walk and rapped on the door, which was instantly pulled open. Natalie blinked as she found herself eye-to-eye with a bargain-basement version of Aunt Lindsay, complete with hair that had seen one perm too many and impossibly long red fingernails. Natalie was looking at Tracey Ducet, the woman who claimed to be Lindsay's missing twin. Over Tracey's shoulder, she could see the woman's sleazy boyfriend, Wayne. Lindsay and Frank were there, too.

"Nat, how *are* you?" Tracey gushed, as if they were long-lost friends and not mere acquaintances. She grabbed Natalie in a hug, and Natalie got a powerful whiff of expensive perfume laid on way too thick. "I just dropped in to say hi to my twin." Tracey cast a wounded-looking smile over her shoulder at Lindsay.

Wayne, who was tall and blond and dressed in white duck trousers and a shirt with an alligator on it, forked wheat-colored hair back from his forehead. "Yes. But we really must be on our way." His accent was as affected as Tracey's was down-home.

"Yeah, we gotta go. Ta-ta!" Tracey swept out the door, Wayne in her wake.

The silence in the foyer after their departure said it all.

"What was *that* all about?" Natalie asked at last.

"What do you think?" Frank muttered grimly. "A five-letter word that starts with *m.*"

"She wants money," Lindsay explained. "A small loan from her twin sister, until everything's cleared up and her inheritance comes through."

"Lord." Natalie cast a glance at the ceiling. "What did you tell her?"

"*I* told her no," Frank said.

"Mom!" It was Carter, Lindsay and Frank's six-year-old, calling them from the other room.

"Coming!" Lindsay hooked an arm through Natalie's. "Come on. Let's open a bottle of wine, barbecue our burgers, and forget what just happened."

Out on the back deck, Natalie helped eight-year-old Chelsea set the table while Frank barbecued hamburgers on a big gas grill. They drank their wine and ate their food to the hissing accompaniment of the electric bug-zappers Frank had mounted around the deck as a defense against the mosquitoes that could eat a person alive on summer evenings at the lake.

After the meal, Frank took Chelsea and Carter into Travistown for ice cream. Since the housekeeper had taken the weekend off, Lindsay and Natalie cleaned up the kitchen.

The talk, as Natalie had pretty much expected it would, turned to the problems in the family. Lindsay was worried about her big brother, Jake.

"Whenever I call him, he tells me not to drop by. He's

too busy. Or he's just going out. Any excuse to put me off. But I saw him in Travistown just yesterday, Nat. He walked right by me." Lindsay bent to put another plate in the dishwasher. "I had to call to him three times before he heard me. And then, for a minute, he looked at me as if he was wondering who I was. And he looks terrible. Red-eyed, hollow-cheeked. As if he hasn't slept in days." She leaned against the counter and folded her slender arms over her chest. "I know he hasn't handled the transition well, since Mother's death. He's made some really bad decisions for the company. And this thing with Monica Malone and the stock he's passed to her..." Lindsay shook her head. "And you know your father. Closed up tight as a bank vault. Thinks he has to handle it all by himself. Your father is and always has been a difficult man to know. But lately, he's impossible. I just hope he's going to be all right."

"Me, too." Natalie pulled out the top tray of the dishwasher and began loading glassware. She'd heard all of this before. And she had nothing to add, nothing helpful to suggest.

"And I feel...so bad, about the Ducet woman." A painful laugh escaped Lindsay. "See? I find it difficult to call her by her first name. And yet...she does look just like me. She really could be my lost twin. But, Nat..."

Natalie looked up and met her aunt's troubled dark eyes. "Say it."

"She's so..."

"Cheap?" Natalie suggested, thinking of the bad perm and the vermillion fingernails.

Lindsay sighed. "You said it, I didn't." She wrinkled her aquiline nose at Natalie. "Am I just a just total snob? Is that it?"

Natalie pushed in the top rack. "No. You are not a

snob. You have every right to feel however you want to feel about Tracey Ducet.''

"I *feel* she's a fake," Lindsay said with heavy irony.

"So does everyone else in the family. Dad has to be having her background investigated."

"You're right. He is."

"I knew it." Natalie remembered the detective Aunt Rebecca had found to look into Grandma Kate's death. "By Gabe Devereax, right?"

"Right. And Gabe is doing what he can. But Tracey has not been helpful. And the couple who raised her are both dead. Gabe can't even come up with a birth certificate on her. She claims she never had one." Lindsay let out a disgusted little snort. "I mean, really. How could any woman reach the age of thirty-seven without having had to produce a birth certificate at least once or twice, to prove who she is?"

"It sounds to me like all you have to do is wait," Natalie said. "Eventually Aunt Rebecca's detective will find out the truth about your supposed long-lost twin." Natalie bent to close the dishwasher, then rose to her height. "And in the meantime, don't give her any money."

"I won't. Don't worry. Frank won't let me."

"Good. Now, look." Natalie took her aunt by the shoulders and pointed her at the open bottle on the counter. "I think there's more wine in that bottle."

"Hmm..." Lindsay said, "I think you're right. Just about exactly two glasses, I'd say."

"Perfect. You pour them. And we'll go back out on the deck and stare at the lake and listen to the bug-zappers offing the mosquitoes and wait for Uncle Frank and the kids to come home."

Lindsay turned back to Natalie and smiled. "Besides

being one of my favorite nieces, you're also a damned good friend.''

"Hey, you know me. Everybody's confidante.''

Lindsay brought out clean glasses and filled them both with wine. "So how's the tenant hunt going?''

"Didn't I tell you? I found him.'' She thought of Rick and wondered, though she knew she shouldn't, how he was getting along back at the house.

"Him?'' Aunt Lindsay asked.

"Yes. He's already moved in. Rick Dalton's his name. A single dad. With an adorable little five-year-old named Toby. Naturally, Toby loves Bernie. And vice versa.''

Lindsay picked up one of the wineglasses and took a small sip. "Okay, so the kid's adorable. And the kid loves the dog and the dog loves the kid. But the question is, what about the single dad. Is *he* adorable?''

"Give me my wine. The lake and the bug-zappers are waiting.''

"I sense romance in the air.''

"Don't say that. Don't even *think* it.''

"But, Nat, why not?'' Lindsay handed Natalie her glass. "You're a total romantic. All your life, you've been looking for true love and a family of your own.''

"All my life, I've been boring.''

Lindsay sipped from her own glass. "That rat Joel Baines really hurt you big-time, didn't he?''

"It wasn't only Joel. It's...everything.''

"Like?''

Natalie thought of Grandma Kate, gone forever now. And her own parents, separated. And all the trouble with Fortune Industries. And her once rock-steady father, who seemed on the verge of some kind of major breakdown. "Let's just go outside. Please?''

"You really don't want to talk about it?''

"Right."

"All right. But you know I'm here, any time."

Natalie thanked her aunt and changed the subject.

Lindsay was scheduled to be at the hospital early the next morning, so they called it a night soon after Frank and the kids returned. It was a little after eight.

Natalie cast about for something to do until ten or eleven. She was hoping that if she stayed out late enough, Rick would be in bed when she got home. But nothing came to mind, beyond finding a bar and ordering a drink, which didn't hold a lot of appeal.

And really, she couldn't spend all her time inventing ways to be somewhere other than her own house. She should either make other arrangements for the next two weeks, or work things out with Rick.

Perhaps a frank talk was called for.

She cringed a little at the thought. She'd spent one afternoon with the man. Surely they hadn't reached the stage of frank talks.

But then she remembered the things they'd said. The subtle electricity in the air when he was near. The kiss that had almost happened.

Yes. The time for a frank talk might be upon them.

He was watching television in the great room off the kitchen when she got home. He looked up and gave her a wave. "Did you have a good time?"

"Yes. Great. Where's Toby?"

"Off to bed."

He went back to his program, leaving Natalie standing in the entrance to the central hall, wondering idiotically whether she felt relieved or disappointed that absolutely nothing out of the ordinary seemed to be going on here.

Bernie, who'd been stretched out at Rick's feet, got up and came over to greet her.

When the dog had been petted, Natalie noticed that there was a message on her machine, which she'd moved to the kitchen now that Toby was in the study. She pushed the play button and there was Joel: "Natalie, all right. If you refuse to give me another chance, well, that is your decision, and I guess I'll have to learn to live with it. But I do have a little problem. Remember that blue Hawaiian-print shirt of mine? Well, I can't find it. I wonder if maybe you could check and see if somehow it ended up with you. I really did love that shirt, Natalie, so I hope you'll be gracious about this and—"

She punched the stop button and reset the machine, silently cursing Joel and his blue Hawaiian-print shirt. Then she shot a quick glance at the back of Rick's head. He seemed oblivious, all wrapped up in his television program. Had he been there, listening in, when Joel called? He'd brought his own cellular phone and answering machine with him; she'd carried the machine into the house when she helped him unload his car. So there was no reason he'd be listening in to her machine.

Unless he'd just happened to be standing nearby when Joel called. She could just see him, standing at the sink, peeling carrots or potatoes or something healthful for his and Toby's dinner, and hearing the machine beep and then Joel's voice—

Natalie scrunched her eyes shut and silently shouted, *Enough!*

She was being truly, disgustingly, ridiculous. And she was stopping it. Now.

"Come on, Bernie," she said, and slapped her thigh. The dog got up from the kitchen floor. "Good night," she called lightly to Rick.

"Good night," Rick said, not turning from his program.

As she climbed the stairs to her own rooms, Natalie decided that a frank talk was the last thing she and Rick Dalton were going to need.

Just to be fair to Joel, before she went to bed, she looked through her closet for his blue Hawaiian print shirt; it wasn't there.

The next day, Sunday, Rick decided to take the *Lady Kate* out again after breakfast. He invited Natalie. She thanked him, but refused.

He asked if maybe he could take Bernie." You know how Toby is about Bernie."

"Sure. Bernie loves to go out on the boat."

"Great. Thanks," Rick said, and that was that.

So Natalie spent the day in the house alone, trying not to think of how lovely it probably was, out on the water. It rained in the afternoon, and she found herself looking out the back windows a lot, expecting to see the *Lady Kate* sliding up to the dock. But two hours passed, the rain stopped and the sun came out, and still the houseboat didn't appear.

Around four, when Rick and Toby had yet to return, Natalie decided to make her favorite chicken-and-broccoli casserole, just to do something constructive with her time.

The casserole was in the oven when the *Lady Kate* appeared at last. Natalie stood at a window in the great room and watched as the houseboat slid into the boathouse.

Ten minutes later, Rick entered through the back door. He looked windblown and suntanned, and Natalie told herself that her heart did not skip a beat at the sight of him. Toby and Bernie trooped in at his heels, headed straight for the central hall.

"Wash your hands, Toby!" Rick called to his son's retreating back. Then, after smiling a greeting at Natalie, he set about putting away the remains of the lunch he'd taken on board with them.

Natalie watched him for a moment, then proposed, very casually, "I've made dinner for all of us, if that's all right with you."

"Sounds terrific—" he sniffed the air "—and smells like heaven. What time do we eat?"

"Forty-five minutes?"

"Let me wash off the layers of bug repellent, and I'll set the table."

"It's a deal." She stared fatuously after him as he disappeared the same way Toby and the dog had gone.

Toby reappeared, Bernie close behind him, just a few minutes after Rick left. Natalie had already cut up the salad, and the rolls were waiting to pop in at the last minute, so she decided to keep busy by getting down the plates and setting out the flatware. When Toby came and sat on a stool nearby, she smiled at him.

He grinned back.

"Time to set the table," she said, in explanation of her actions.

But Toby apparently thought she was giving him instructions. Because he slid down from the stool and picked up the plates. Natalie watched, pleased, as Toby carried the plates to the breakfast table and set them around.

"Excellent," she said, studying the plates and their placement on the table. "Do you know how to do the flatware, glasses and napkins?"

Solemnly Toby shook his head.

She showed him, very slowly setting one place for him, putting each piece where it belonged. "Think you can handle it?"

He nodded. Carefully, his little tongue caught between his teeth, he began the task. When he'd finished, a couple of the utensils had ended up backward, but apart from that it was a fine job.

Natalie was just telling him so when Rick returned. She looked up as he appeared from the hall. "You don't have to set the table. Toby did."

"He what?" Rick's expression showed his disbelief.

"He set the table," Natalie said again. Rick strode to Natalie's side and examined his son's handiwork. Natalie tried not to think how clean and good he smelled, or to pay any attention at all to the way her pulse insisted on acting up at his nearness.

"This is just…"

Natalie could hear the jubilation in his voice, and she put her hand on his arm. He looked at her.

"Good," she said evenly. "It's good."

He took her cue that he shouldn't go overboard about it. "Yeah," he agreed after a moment. "It's good."

With a shy, pleased smile, Toby turned away from them and headed for the great room, where he switched on the television and stretched out on the rug in front of it. Bernie, who'd been sitting by the breakfast table while Toby set the places, got up and went to lie beside the boy.

"You're a miracle worker," Rick whispered in her ear.

His praise warmed her, while the caress of his breath against her skin sent shivers singing along every nerve ending she possessed. She suggested, "Maybe Toby's ready to take on a few chores around the house."

"Maybe he is."

They grinned at each other. And then she realized she was still holding his arm. She let go and jumped back as if touching him burned her.

He stared at her in obvious bewilderment. "What's the matter?"

She knew then that even if Rick didn't need that frank talk she kept pondering having with him, *she* did.

"We have to talk." There. She had said it.

He didn't seem the least bit surprised. "When?"

"Tonight. After Toby's in bed."

"Are you...interested in me—as a woman, I mean?"

Rick, who was sitting at the other end of the couch from her in the great room, stared at her for a moment. Then, grimly, he answered, "Yes."

She sighed. "I thought so."

"You don't want me to be interested? Is that what this is about?"

Her heart cried, *Oh, but I do!* She told it to shut up. "I don't want to get involved with anyone right now. I really don't."

He watched her for another endless moment, his blue eyes hooded in the lamplight. "Because of the guy with the Hawaiian shirt?"

She let out a little groan. "You *did* hear that message."

"I was standing at the sink—"

"Peeling carrots, right?"

"Washing lettuce, I think it was."

"Whatever." She folded her hands in her lap and looked down at them. "That was Joel."

"Your ex, right? The one you told me about yesterday, who broke it off with you a month ago."

"Right. Recently, though, he changed his mind and wanted to work things out. I don't. Not with anybody. I want...some time on my own."

"I see."

She looked up, desperate for him to understand. "Oh, Rick. When you came to see the house that day, I was so happy. And I liked you so much. And Toby, too. I knew that I'd found just the right people to live here with Bernie while I was gone. I didn't realize..." She had no idea how to go on.

He did it for her. "That you liked me in more ways than one."

"I..."

"Come on, Natalie. It's there in the air, every time we look at each other. Are you going to try to tell me it's only coming from me?"

She longed to say yes, but she just couldn't get her mouth around a lie that big. "No."

"You feel something for me, too, then?"

"I... Yes."

"But you don't want to act on it."

"It's just...too sudden for me. It's not what I'm looking for."

"And what *are* you looking for?"

She threw up both hands. "That's just it. I don't exactly know. Lately, my whole world seems so crazy. Turned upside down. If you read the newspaper or turn on the news, you know what a mess my family's in. And then there's my personal life. I really thought I loved Joel. But after he broke it off, I started to see that it had been more habit than anything else. I thought that I was *safe* with him. He depended on me. Needed me, I thought, and I... Oh, you don't want to hear this, do you?"

He seemed to be studying her face. When he spoke, his voice was carefully reasonable. "You're confused."

"Major understatement."

Now he was the one sighing. "At least you're being honest with me." He rubbed the back of his neck. "So what do we do?"

"I could...move across the lake, until it's time for me to leave."

"The prospect doesn't seem to thrill you."

"It doesn't. Things are pretty grim over there, and I'm trying to stay out of the problems my family is having. But I could do it, and I'd be willing to do it, if that was what you wanted. Or I could check into a hotel for a while."

"There's another option. Toby and I could leave."

She met his eyes. "No. Really. I don't want that. I have this feeling that this is the place Toby should be right now. And you're still the perfect tenants. Except for this...*thing* between you and me."

"I agree with you—about Toby, at least. And right now, in my life, Toby's what matters most."

"Then you do want to stay?"

"Yeah. And you *don't* want to go?"

"No, not unless I have to."

"So what do we do, then?"

"Well..."

"Say it."

"All right. I was thinking that we could give avoidance a try."

"Avoidance?"

"Yes. I'll do my best to stay out of your way."

"No more chicken-and-broccoli casseroles?" He looked wistful.

"Right. Since you're renting the place, you have priority. I'll work around you. I'll either eat out or use the kitchen when you're not.''

He shook his head. ''I don't know about this.''

''Let's give it a chance, at least. And if it doesn't work out, I'll find somewhere else to stay.''

Later, in bed, Rick told himself he was better off knowing up front that Natalie Fortune had no idea what she wanted from life—except that it *wasn't* him.

He supposed he'd been wrong about her from the first. She wasn't his fantasy girl-next-door come to life, after all. She was a very confused woman. She'd said it herself.

Unfortunately, he couldn't seem to get certain images out of his mind. Images of Natalie, dressed in spangles and sequins, singing ''Piece of My Heart'' at the top of her lungs. And smiling at Toby, that very first time, when Toby had smiled back. And yesterday, on the front lawn, in old cutoffs, with her hair in a falling-down ponytail, a fine dew of sweat making her smooth skin gleam…

Rick groaned and turned over and tried to ignore the fact that he was aroused again.

He was playing the fool. Getting sentimental—and totally turned on—over a woman who'd just told him to keep away from her.

He gritted his teeth and pictured the scale drawings of the shopping mall he'd been working on just before he took the summer off. He re-created on the screen of his mind each and every line of those damn blueprints, until there was nothing left of his desire but a sore jaw from clenching it so hard.

It would work out all right, he told himself. He'd stay clear of Natalie Fortune as much as possible, as they'd agreed. Because the last damn thing he needed in his life

right now was some confused little rich girl playing
games with his mind.

It was some time after eleven when he finally managed
to fall asleep. And it seemed like only moments later that
Toby's terrified screams had him shooting bolt upright
and shoving the covers back.

Six

Rick raced for the door that connected his room to his son's room. Once there, he flicked the wall switch.

Toby shrieked.

Rick blinked against the sudden glare, then forced his eyes open and scanned the room. The bed with the airplane spread was empty, the covers all tangled. In a corner, across the room, Toby cowered, scrunched into a tight ball, knees drawn up, head down.

"Toby." Rick tried to speak calmly, though his heart was racing and his blood was roaring so strongly in his ears that it seemed almost loud enough to compete with Toby's anguished wails. "Toby, listen. Toby, it's Daddy. Toby, it's okay." Cautiously Rick approached.

Toby seemed to cower down into himself, growing ever smaller, until he was little more than a pitiful knot of sharp elbows and thin ankles and knobby knees and rumpled Snoopy pajamas. He shook, his head still buried against his knees, unwilling to look up.

"Oh, Toby…" Total helplessness washed over Rick, as it did every time this happened. He wanted to shield and protect.

And yet the demons were inside his son's mind. How could Rick protect Toby from that?

Dr. Dawkins had said Rick should "Offer comfort. *Be* there for Toby when the nightmares strike. Above all, don't overreact yourself. Be calm. Show him everything's okay by how okay you are."

It all sounded great. The only problem was, when this happened, Rick just didn't feel particularly okay. He felt powerless and angry. He wanted to *fight* those demons. He wanted to smash them to dust.

He drew in a calming breath and let it out slowly, then dropped into a crouch before his son. He reached out. "Toby..."

Toby gave a frightened cry and pressed himself tighter against the wall.

"Toby, son..."

Toby dared to look up. His eyes were blue pools of stark fear. He hunched his shoulders and pointed beyond Rick's shoulder. Rick looked back and saw nothing but the door to the room's small closet, slightly ajar.

He turned to his son again and found that Toby had buried his head against his knees once more. Rick hadn't the faintest idea what to do next. "Oh, Toby..."

And then he heard Natalie's soft voice. "Rick."

He whipped his head around. She was standing in the door to the central hall, wearing a white terry-cloth robe. Her slender feet were bare, and her hair was loose and tangled around her face. The bright overhead light reflected off the gold chain around her neck, and made the rosebud charm seem to glow. The big dog stood slightly behind her, out in the hall.

Rick forgot all about the things she'd said to him earlier in the evening. All he felt was thankful that she had come, that she would help. He didn't doubt for a second that she would know what to do.

He rose to his feet and stepped aside as she came to take his place before Toby, crouching down as he himself had done. Bernie crossed the threshold and then sat just inside the door.

Rick watched what she did.

She didn't try to touch Toby right away. She just spoke, very slowly and deliberately.

"Tell me, Toby. Tell me what it is."

Still quivering, Toby lifted his head.

"Tell me," she said again.

Toby looked at her for the longest time. And then his lips silently shaped a single word.

Monster.

"Where?" Natalie asked.

He looked beyond her shoulder, to the closet door. And then, his hand shaking a little, he raised it and pointed his finger where he looked.

Bernie growled. Rick glanced at the big, normally friendly dog, and saw he was baring his teeth at the closet door.

Rick looked back at his son, who had stopped shaking and was staring in wide-eyed adoration at the dog.

Natalie chose that moment to reach out. "Come here. Come on." With a hungry little cry, Toby surged into her open arms.

Holding him tight against her body, whispering words of comfort, she stood. "Listen. You're safe. Your dad's here. And Bernie. And me, too. We won't let that monster get you. Never. Never in a million years." She stroked and patted and crooned soothing promises as she carried him to the bed and sat down, settling him in her lap. Bernie padded immediately over to the edge of the bed, where he nuzzled Toby's leg.

When the boy reached out to touch the dog, Natalie looked up and signaled Rick to turn off the harsh overhead light. She switched on the airplane lamp at the same

time. The softer light was a welcome change, Rick realized.

Natalie edged Toby off her lap and then waved Rick
over to sit next to him on his other side. Then, when they
sat in a row on the edge of the bed, with Bernie at their
feet, she asked, "Was the monster in the closet, Toby, is
that it?"

The boy shivered and leaned close to her. She put her
arm around him. Rick saw him nod.

She stroked Toby's hair. "You know there really are
no monsters, don't you, Toby?"

Toby knew no such thing; he shook his head vehe-
mently.

"Okay, I admit," Natalie confessed, "My grandpa
Ben always said there was a monster at the bottom of
Lake Travis. But it was a *friendly* monster."

That got Toby's attention. He pulled back and stared
at her, wide-eyed.

"You didn't know there were friendly monsters,
Toby?"

Solemnly Toby shook his head.

"Well, in my experience, that's the only kind there
are."

Toby looked at her. It seemed to Rick that he desperately wanted to believe, but somehow didn't quite dare.

"Hey," she said. "How would you like it if Bernie
slept in here with you?" She glanced at Rick. "If your
dad says it's okay, that is."

Rick agreed without a second's hesitation. "No problem for me."

Natalie looked at Toby again. "Well?"

Toby's nod was quick and eager.

"Okay, then. It's settled." She stood. "And I'm going
back to my own bed, where I belong. Good night, Toby."

Toby nodded.

Natalie straightened her robe and patted her dog on the head. "Stay."

And then she turned to go.

Rick couldn't stop himself. "Natalie."

She paused and gave him one last look. He met her eyes, trying to communicate in a glance exactly how damn grateful he was, not caring at all that he probably reminded her of Toby gazing in adoration and wonder at her Saint Bernard. "Thanks."

She granted him a tiny smile and a nod. And then she was gone.

As Rick tucked Toby in again, he told himself that Natalie Fortune could turn away from the attraction between them from now until doomsday—he'd be forever grateful for what she was doing to help Toby.

Meanwhile, out in the central hall, Natalie paused at the foot of the stairs, tempted to linger and speak with Rick just a little when he was through in Toby's room. But then she recalled too clearly the sight of him a moment ago, wearing nothing but a pair of pajama bottoms and looking at her as if she had single-handedly saved the world from destruction.

No, the last thing she should do right now was to hang around for another word with him. With a sigh of regret, she mounted the stairs.

The next day, Monday, Rick and Natalie were cordial with each other at breakfast time. No casual observer would have noticed the subtle tension between them.

Toby came to the table and ate heartily. Rick couldn't help thinking that, in the few days they'd been at the farmhouse, Toby had begun to seem more and more like a normal, healthy little boy. Except for his continuing silence, of course. And the occasional forays into tight spaces. And the nightmare last night.

But the nightmares really weren't as frequent as they'd once been. And Toby did eat better now. And sometimes, now, he smiled. His face had more animation in it.

Dr. Hawkins had said that these things would happen, that Toby was coming along fine. Until lately, though, it had been hard for Rick to believe it.

Until Natalie. And her dog.

In fact, it had occurred to Rick after he crawled back into his bed last night that without Natalie and the dog, Toby could end up right back where he started: isolated inside himself, unable—or unwilling—to reach out.

Natalie would be gone just exactly two weeks from now. The dog would be around until the end of August. But when Toby and Rick returned to Minneapolis, the dog would stay behind. Toby's weekly visit with Dr. Dawkins was scheduled for two that afternoon. Rick decided he'd have to share his concern with the psychiatrist, and see what she said about it.

In the meantime, he looked across the table at his landlady and tried not to think about the creamy softness of her skin in the morning light, or the tender shadows beneath her eyes that made him wonder if she'd slept as little as he had last night.

After breakfast, Rick took Toby out to the dock for a while. They played at fishing with a couple of ancient poles Rick had found in the boathouse. When pretending to fish got old, they wandered back inside and settled down in the great room with a Teenage Mutant Ninja Turtles puzzle. Rick was showing Toby a few tricks for putting a puzzle together when the Saint Bernard, who was flopped comfortably nearby, suddenly lifted his head and growled—the same growl he'd given the monster in the closet the night before.

The knock at the glass-topped back door came seconds later. Rick looked up and met the eyes of the visitor through the glass: another man, one close to Rick's age. Rick guessed immediately that it must be Joel, the old boyfriend.

Natalie was upstairs by then—keeping that low profile she'd been so insistent about the night before.

"Look for more pieces of Rafael's shell," Rick advised Toby, as he got to his feet from his cross-legged position on the rug at the wide, low coffee table.

When he got to the door, he judged that the visitor was just an inch or two under his own six-foot-two. And aside from a slightly weak chin, he was a good-looking man.

Rick pulled open the door. "Yes?"

"Is...Natalie here?"

Rick tried not to take too much pleasure in the guy's discomfort at finding another man in the house. "She's upstairs, I think." He held out his hand. "I'm Rick Dalton. You're Joel, right?"

"Yes. I'm Joel." Joel acquiesced to a handshake. "Natalie didn't mention she had company." Over by the coffee table, Bernie growled again. Joel sent the dog a tight frown.

Rick smiled broadly. "Listen, I'll go and get her."

Joel coughed. "Well. Thanks."

"Hey, no problem." He stepped back a little. "Come on in."

Bernie was up on all four huge paws now. He actually seemed to be glaring at Joel. Toby was watching the other man too, his small, pointed face pinched up in a scowl; if Bernie had his doubts about this guy, then Toby wanted nothing to do with him, either.

"Uh, no," Joel said. "I'll just wait right out here on the porch."

"Suit yourself."

Natalie appeared from the central hall just as Rick turned to go and get her.

"Joel." Her tone was far from friendly.

Joel coughed again. "Natalie, it's really important to me that we talk. If you would only—"

She shoved the empty coffee cup she was carrying onto the kitchen counter. "Fine." Then she flew across the room and grabbed Joel by the arm. "Outside." She stepped over the threshold and closed the door behind them.

Rick resolutely did not look out the bank of windows at Natalie and her uninvited guest. He went back to his son and the puzzle and the sensitive, insightful, old-boyfriend-eating dog.

Outside, Natalie said, "Joel, I do not have your shirt. I do not have anything that belongs to you. So please leave me alone."

Joel looked down at his shoes. "All right. It's not really about the shirt." He looked up and peered through one of the windows, his brow furrowing. "Who is that?"

"My tenant. And his little boy. Not that it's any of your business."

"A tenant? Why do you need a tenant?"

"Joel. You've got until a count of five."

"All right. I just wanted you to know, I'm getting married."

Natalie blinked. She had no idea what to say to that.

Which gave Joel time to continue. "Remember those 'slight unfaithfulnesses' I mentioned?"

"Joel, I don't see what this has to do with—"

"Well, the truth is, the woman I was unfaithful to you

with wasn't as careful as she should have been. And now, I'm going to be a dad. Naturally, I want to do what's right.''

Natalie forced herself to speak, before he could tell her something else that she had no desire whatsoever to hear. ''What in the world does this have to do with me?''

''I just... You were always such a good *listener,* Natalie. And I've missed that. You can't know how much. It meant a lot to me. To tell you all that I was going through. To get your feedback. You always seemed to know just the right thing to say. Melissa—that's the woman who's going to have my baby—is beautiful and lots of fun. But she's very demanding. She exhausts me, you know? I miss the quiet times you and I used to share. I'd like nothing more than the chance to share times like that with you again.''

''Wait a minute.'' Natalie spoke very slowly, very clearly. ''Let me get this straight. You've made a woman pregnant. And you're going to marry her. But you still want to keep on seeing me. Is that right?''

''Well...'' He drew in a deep breath. ''I don't know. I don't know what I want, exactly. But I *miss* you, Natalie. I miss you terribly. And yesterday, when Melissa told me about the baby, I found that all I could think of was calling you, talking it over with you, seeing if you had any advice for me. I realize that *romantically,* you're probably through with me. And that's okay. I can learn to live with that. If we could just be friends, Natalie. Friends, please. That's all I'm asking.''

Natalie realized that her mouth was hanging open. She snapped it shut. She longed to be able to tell herself that this wasn't actually happening. But it was.

''Joel, do I have *Welcome* written across my chest?''

''What are you talking about? Of course not.''

"Then why is it you feel compelled to wipe your feet on me?"

"Natalie. Don't be foolish. I only want to *talk* to you, to tell you—"

"Joel. If you ever come near me again, I will call the police. Do you understand?"

"But, Natalie—"

"I'm going inside now. If you do not leave immediately, I will call the police *right now*."

Joel dragged in a big breath to argue some more, but then something in her expression must have reached him at last. He peered at her, frowning. "You really mean it, don't you?"

"I do."

He shook his head. "You never want to see me again." His voice dripped disbelief—and unwilling acceptance.

"Bingo."

"Well." He blinked a few times, and forked his light brown hair back from his high forehead. "All right. I guess I'll...go."

"Thank you." She stood there on the porch, watching him, until he disappeared back around toward the front of the house, where he must have parked his car. She was reasonably certain, from the look of stunned understanding she'd seen on his face, that he wouldn't be bothering her anymore. For that much, she was grateful.

But she still couldn't help wondering grimly what was wrong with her judgment, for her to have been involved with Joel Baines in the first place.

"Natalie?"

She turned to see Rick, standing in the door behind her, looking achingly handsome in the old pair of sweatpants and black T-shirt he'd been wearing since breakfast. "Everything okay?" He sounded honestly concerned.

Her heart—which couldn't be trusted—was suddenly beating faster. "Yes. Everything's fine. Joel and I had a little...misunderstanding. But I think it's cleared up at last."

"Glad to hear it." The words seemed to have a hundred dangerous meanings. And he was smiling at her. That was dangerous, too.

Remember Joel, she thought bleakly. *Remember that you have absolutely no judgment when it comes to men. Remember that you are maintaining a low profile around here.*

"I'll just get a little more coffee," she said distantly. "And go back to my rooms."

His smile faded to nothing. He stepped back. "After you." His tone was cool.

She granted him a distant smile, and went ahead of him into the house.

Seven

That afternoon in Minneapolis, after Dr. Dawkins met with Toby, she invited Rick into her private office for a short consultation.

The doctor was pleased. "Toby's doing wonderfully. He makes direct eye contact. He even smiled twice during our visit today. The period of withdrawal he suffered through is almost completely over, I believe. Watch for him to start talking again soon. And when he does, don't make too much of it. He might say a word or two, and then not talk again for a while. Don't push him. Let him rediscover his voice in his own way." She sat back in her big leather chair and templed her fingers. "Also, I think it's time to cut back to two appointments per month."

Rick felt a surge of pure elation. And then he thought of Natalie and the dog.

"Is there something on your mind, Mr. Dalton?"

"As a matter of fact, yes." He explained about his new landlady and the dog that Toby adored. "Toby smiled the first moment he met her. And she leaves for a trip in two weeks. And Toby is nuts about that dog. We're watching the dog while the landlady's gone. But when Toby and I return home in the fall, the dog will stay behind. I'm concerned."

"That he'll regress without them?"

"Yes. That's it, exactly."

There was a gleam in the doctor's dark eyes. "Don't worry."

"But—"

"Mr. Dalton, let me remind you that *you* are the central figure here. It is your commitment, your *investment* of time and attention in Toby, that is making the difference for him. As long as his relationship with you remains stable, he will continue to improve. I have no doubt at all that the day will come, not too long from today, when you will look at your son and see a perfectly normal, healthy, happy little boy. The nice landlady and the friendly dog can help, and you may see a few signs of worrisome past behaviors when Toby loses contact with them. But it won't devastate him. He'll get past it. *You* are the person with whom he is bonding. And as long as you keep showing him your love and commitment, he will be all right."

Rick rubbed his eyes.

"I know," the doctor said, "it's a huge responsibility." She chuckled. "But you're doing great so far."

He thought of Natalie, the night before, knowing exactly what to say to Toby about the monster in the closet—when Rick himself hadn't had a clue. He shook his head. "I'm glad you think I'm doing all right. But sometimes, I'm not so sure."

"Be sure. You are doing fine."

"Sometimes I think that what I need is a wife." The words were out before he even realized he would say them.

Dr. Dawkins was silent for a moment before she advised, "You do not *need* a wife, Mr. Dalton. Not as far as Toby is concerned. However—" now there was a grin on her smooth ebony face "—if you *want* a wife, that's another issue entirely." She rose from her chair. "I think we're through for the day."

Rick stood, as well. Dr. Dawkins came around her desk and showed him to the door, reminding him to schedule Toby's next appointment on the way out.

When Toby and Rick returned to the farmhouse, there was a white Mercedes parked in front. Rick pulled around by the side door, planning to unload the groceries he'd bought.

Before he and Toby could get out of the car, Natalie appeared in the doorway to the small, enclosed side porch. Bernie slid around her and bounded down the steps. Rick gave him a quick pat on his broad flank as the dog went past, headed for the real object of his affections: Toby.

While Toby greeted the dog, Rick stared at Natalie, wondering what her distracted expression might mean and trying not to think about how good it made him feel just to see her standing in a doorway in shorts and a faded blue shirt. Her hair, as usual, was escaping from her ponytail.

"Thought I'd bring in the groceries through the closest door this time."

The frown between her brows melted away, and she said teasingly, "You brought half a grocery store with you when you first arrived. That was only the day before yesterday."

Rick said nothing, only unlatched the trunk with the button in the glove compartment and then got out of the car. He was wondering how this could be happening to him. He'd met the woman two weeks ago, and this was only the third day he'd spent in her house. She'd made him promise to keep his distance. And yet, every time he laid eyes on her, all he wanted was to get closer.

When he glanced at Natalie again, he saw that her teasing smile had faded—probably because she'd remembered their little agreement, which she seemed to have the same tendency to forget as he did.

In a businesslike tone, she volunteered, "I'll help you." She started for the trunk of the car.

He beat her there. "No need. I'll handle it."

She stopped halfway between him and the house. "I don't mind."

He threw the trunk lid all the way up. "I said, I'll handle it."

"Of course." She took a step backward. He could see in her eyes that his harsh tone had hurt her. He felt like a jerk.

"Natalie?" The hesitant, well-modulated voice came from the door to the porch.

Rick looked up to see Grace Kelly, dressed all in white, standing in the porch doorway where Natalie had stood a moment ago. He blinked and then looked again. On that second glance, he decided he wasn't seeing ghosts after all. This woman's oval face was a little narrower and her body slimmer than the fabled princess of Monaco's had been. But she was every bit as stunningly beautiful, a fully mature woman who might have been anywhere from thirty-five to fifty.

"I'm coming, Mother." Natalie turned and started for the house again.

The beautiful blonde smiled at him over her daughter's head. "Hello. I'm Erica. Natalie's mom."

"Rick Dalton, the tenant."

"A pleasure."

Natalie hooked her arm through her mother's. "Let's go in, Mom. Rick wants to get his things unloaded."

But Erica Fortune pulled away. "Natalie, I'm sure he doesn't mind taking a moment to say hello. And I do want to meet the child."

Toby, who had already noticed the strange woman, now approached cautiously, Bernie at his side.

"Hello." The vision in white stepped lightly down the short porch steps and knelt in the grass, her snowy skirt belling out around her like the petals of some delicate flower. "I'm Erica." She smiled a tender smile, and suddenly Rick could see the resemblance between mother and daughter.

Toby shyly smiled back.

"His name is Toby," Natalie said.

"I know. You told me." Erica Fortune's attention was all on Toby. "I had a little boy. Only one. Now he's all grown up, with children of his own and, at last, a lovely, good wife."

Toby reached out and stroked the woman's silvery-blond hair, which gleamed in the sun like platinum spun with gold. She laughed, a laugh like Natalie's, only slightly more brittle and not quite so warm. And then she grabbed Toby and hugged him.

Rick took one protective step forward; Toby was very reserved, as a rule. He might be frightened.

But then he saw that Toby was allowing the embrace. More than allowing it, actually; he was wrapping his thin arms around Natalie's mother. He was patting Erica's back.

Erica was the one who pulled away. Sighing, she rose lightly to her feet. "You're an angel," she said to Toby. She looked up at Rick, and he saw that her green eyes were moist. "I love children," she said. "Sometimes I miss the days when mine were small. Life seems so...tenuous sometimes lately. Then, things were simpler. Or at least it seems so now.''

Natalie spoke from the steps. ''Come on, Mom. Let's go up to my rooms and—''

''No, really. You've already done what you always do. Listened. And cared. I feel much better. So I'll be on my way.''

''Are you sure?''

''Positive. Nice to meet you, Rick.'' She granted him a gracious smile, then spoke to her daughter again. ''Walk me to the car.''

As the two women started for the front of the house, Rick reached for the bags in the trunk. And then he saw his son out of the corner of his eye, heading around back to play with the dog. It occurred to him that a boy who was up to hugging a woman he'd never met before was probably ready to help carry in the groceries.

''Hey, Toby!''

Toby stopped and turned.

''I could use a little help here.''

Toby made a face.

''I mean it. Come on.''

Dragging his feet, slumping his shoulders—in short, looking very much like the average little boy—Toby did what Rick told him to do.

Inside, Rick saw the tabloid newspaper spread open on the breakfast table. Curious, he slid the bags he was carrying onto a counter and went to look at the thing.

Monica Malone and Ben Fortune, the headline read, Their secret love that lasted a quarter of a century. The words were splashed across separate photographs of the beauty queen and a handsome gray-haired man, the late

Ben Fortune. Worse, the shots had been spliced together to make it look as if the actress were about to kiss the former head of the Fortune empire.

There was a shot of Kate Fortune, too, off to the side. She wore a disapproving expression on her patrician face, one that had probably been aimed at whatever determined member of the paparazzi had snapped the picture. But, of course, the tabloid wanted the reader to think that Kate's expression showed distress at what was going on between her husband and the former goddess of the silver screen.

The whole thing was cheap and exploitative—and most likely not true. But still, Rick was curious. He started to read the story, but only got through the first few lines before a loaf of bread hit the table at his elbow. He glanced up from the page to meet his son's challenging eyes.

Can I go play now? the boy's expression said.

"Go out and bring in that bag of potatoes and the box of laundry detergent. And then you can play."

Toby wrinkled his pug nose.

"Go on. Do it."

Toby trudged out, Bernie close behind.

Rick turned back to the magazine. He scanned the lines quickly. There was nothing to substantiate the outrageous charge at all. The piece began with "An informed source has revealed…" and didn't have much more to say than the shocking headline, except to propose the theory that Monica Malone's recent acquisition of so much Fortune Industries stock might be her way of getting even with the Fortune family.

"Though the legendary Monica Malone was the one great and true love of Ben Fortune's life, he would never give up his wife and his family for her. So they shared their love in the shadows. And now, at last, Monica Malone is stepping forward, demanding that the Fortune family deal with her, claiming her own place in the sun...."

The rest was a recap of Kate and Ben Fortune's accomplishments during their lifetimes, as well as a list of the films Monica Malone had made in her long career. Toby came in as Rick finished reading. He was lugging the potatoes, which he dropped on the floor just inside the door. Then, with a loud sigh, he turned to go back for the detergent.

Rick grinned at his retreating back. "Hey, wait for me."

Toby shot him a put-upon look as Rick hurried to catch up with him.

Rick was sliding his third and last load of groceries onto the counter and Toby was already outside playing when Natalie appeared. Rick watched from the corner of his eye as she went straight to the table, where the tabloid was waiting, and scooped the thing up. When she turned for the hall, her gaze collided with his.

Her brows drew together, and he knew that *she* knew what he'd been doing while she was telling her mother goodbye.

"You read this," she said accusingly.

"Guilty." He carried the bag of produce he'd bought over to the fridge and knelt to start putting the vegetables away in the crisper drawer.

Natalie didn't move. A glance or two over his shoulder showed him that she was rolling the tabloid into a tube. She hit it once against the edge of the table. "My mother brought it over. She's very upset. She loathes stuff like this."

"I can understand why. It's totally exploitative and, ten to one, a complete fabrication."

"You think so?"

He spared her another glance. She looked so hopeful—and so damned adorable.

"If I were you, I'd have told your mother not to waste her time worrying about uncorroborated garbage."

She chuckled. "I think I said something along those lines."

"Good." He stood to pull a head of lettuce from the grocery bag on the counter, and then paused to give her a smile. She smiled tentatively back. He found he didn't want to break eye contact with her long enough to bend and put the lettuce away. So he just stood there, with the refrigerator door open, holding the lettuce, looking at her while she looked back at him, both of them smiling like the fools they probably were.

But then she caught herself. She hit the rolled-up paper against her palm. "Well. I should get on upstairs."

Rick said nothing, only bent to put the lettuce where it belonged.

In the apartment Sterling had found for her when she first went into hiding, Kate sat at a small desk in the skylighted living room, the tabloid paper spread out in front of her.

Sterling was pacing the room, waiting for her to finish reading the disgusting thing.

When she looked up from the page, he froze in mid-stride. Their eyes met.

"Kate..." Sterling began, and then didn't seem to know what to say next.

Kate looked down at her own hands, which she'd folded on top of the ridiculous doctored pictures of her husband and Monica Malone. Over the decades, Kate had suspected that there might be something between Monica and Ben. Especially during the worst years of her marriage, those years when Kate's first real success with Fortune Cosmetics had left Ben feeling threatened by her growing independence. But their marriage had lasted, and Kate knew Ben had loved her deeply.

Still, there had been little signs. Tiny things. Things that only a woman who knows a man to his soul would have noticed: a subject avoided, a shifted glance, a knowing look across a crowded room.

But Kate had never set about finding out for sure whether her husband was betraying her with the woman she herself had chosen to be the first Fortune's Face. Maybe she hadn't wanted to know.

It occurred to her that if anyone besides the legendary film star herself might know the truth, it would be Sterling. As Kate trusted him, so had Ben—implicitly.

She dared to ask, "Do you think it's true?"

Sterling's eyes gave nothing away. "I don't know."

"But you heard the rumors, too, over the years? You saw the...indications?"

He coughed—and then muttered a low, reluctant "Yes."

She spoke crisply. "All right, then. I want to find out who leaked this. Whoever it was might have information about the larger picture."

"I know. And I'll get right on it. The possibilities, unfortunately, are endless. A disgruntled employee of some branch of Fortune Industries. An eager reporter willing to stoop so low as fabricating a story out of whole cloth. Or someone totally unconnected—a waiter or a shop owner—who happened to spot the Malone woman and Ben together."

"I get the idea. What about Tracey Ducet, or that boyfriend of hers?"

"We'll check into them."

"Or even Monica herself."

"As I said, we'll do all we can. I'll put Gabe Devereax on it right away."

"All right, then." Kate stood from the desk. "Now, I suppose, we should talk about Jake."

Sterling's expression was grim. "I went to see him, as you requested. Yesterday, at nine in the morning, at the estate."

"And?"

"What can I say? It turned out just as I warned you it would. He was distant and polite and got rid of me as quickly as he could without being blatantly rude."

"Did you find out anything about his connection with Monica Malone, about what the woman might have on him, that he would turn over so much stock to her?"

Sterling looked at her patiently. "He didn't let me get within a hundred miles of that subject."

"But…how is he? How does he *seem?*"

"Kate…"

"There's something. I can see it in those eyes of yours. Tell me."

Sterling hesitated another endless few seconds before confessing, "He'd been drinking."

"At nine in the morning?"

"Yes. He looked very bad, Kate."

Kate went to the window, which had been specially treated so that no prying eyes could see in, and stood looking out, westward, toward the suburb of Golden Valley. "This thing has to break open soon. I feel it."

"You've been right about so much, Kate. Let's hope to God you're right now."

Eight

Carrying one small bag with a few scandalously revealing scraps of lingerie in it, Natalie let herself in the side door. The day had been hot, and she felt sticky and uncomfortable. And though she'd left for the city early, with plans to shop until the soles of her shoes wore thin, she found her heart wasn't in it. That was why, after she'd bought the lingerie, she'd frittered away a couple of hours in a window seat at a deli, watching the people go by and nibbling a corned beef on rye. Then she'd wandered into a movie theater and watched a Disney double bill: *Pocahontas* and *Cinderella.* That had cheered her a little. Natalie loved Disney movies. She'd walked out of the theater singing "Bibbity, Bobbity, Boo" under her breath.

However, her spirits didn't stay lifted for long. Traffic had been a bear coming home. And she'd found herself wondering why she'd left in the first place.

But, of course, she knew why. Because of her low profile that she had to keep to achieve her two-week goal of staying away from Rick.

And then it came to her that if there *were* no Rick, she'd have probably gone shopping today anyway. Because shopping a lot was part of her effort to be frivolous and decadent for a change.

And that depressed her, for some stupid reason.

She heard Rick's voice coming from the front parlor

the minute she slipped through the door. It was a deep voice, just a little bit velvety. And very warm.

She stood still, listening. He was reading a story. She couldn't help herself. She tiptoed through the dining room and stood in the open arch that led to the parlor.

Rick and Toby were sitting close together on the sofa, a good-size picture book spread midway between their two sets of knees. Bernie was sprawled at their feet, his head on his paws. Natalie wished she was sitting there with them, listening to Rick read a story in the air-conditioned parlor on a hot afternoon.

The boy, the dog and the man all looked up at the same time.

Natalie put on a bright smile. "Hi there."

Bernie dragged himself upright and lumbered over for a few pats of greeting. Toby just grinned.

"We're reading *Aladdin*," Rick explained.

She could see the pictures from where she stood. "The Disney version?" She couldn't quite keep the wistfulness out of her voice.

"Yep," Rick said, then frowned as something occurred to him. "Listen. You got a message about an hour ago. It sounded important. Maybe you ought to—"

She thought of her father, who was so unstable lately. And her perpetually distraught mother. And the thousand other weird things that had been going on with the people she loved in recent months. "Thanks." Her heartbeat suddenly loud and hollow in her ears, she headed back toward the kitchen.

As Rick had warned her, the message light was blinking on her answering machine. She tossed the bag of lingerie on the counter, went around the end of it and over to the side where the machine was waiting. She pressed the play button.

And the soft British voice that she'd heard once before said, "Hello. This is Jessica Holmes again. I called several days ago. And I had sincerely hoped I might hear back from you. As I said then, it concerns a Benjamin Fortune, who would be in his seventies now, and who served in France during the Second World War. Just in case you didn't receive my first message... Please. If you or anyone you know is a blood relative of this man, it is imperative that you get back to me. I don't want to be an alarmist, and it's impossible to explain over the phone, but this truly is a matter of life and death. Thank you." Once again, before she hung up, she left a London phone number.

"Well?"

Natalie looked up to see Rick standing near the entrance to the laundry alcove. He'd followed her through the dining room to see what she was going to do about that "important" call.

She pressed the reset button.

Rick swore under his breath. "You're not even going to call the woman back?"

Natalie said nothing as the machine whirred and clicked.

Rick crossed the kitchen, stopping on the other side of the counter from where she stood. "'Life and death,' the woman said. 'A matter of life and death.'"

Natalie mentally counted to ten. She reminded herself that Rick didn't come from a wealthy, well-known family. He had no idea of the utter shamelessness of a reporter on the scent of a big story.

"Natalie. Call her back."

"This does not concern you." With some effort, she kept her tone level.

"Yes, it does. Any matter of life and death concerns me. As it should concern you."

"It isn't a matter of life and death."

"How do you know, unless you call her back and talk to her?"

"I know. All the signs are there."

"What signs?"

"Oh, Rick..."

"Don't roll your eyes at me. What signs?"

Natalie simply did not feel like going into it. She tried switching subjects. "Where are Toby and Bernie?"

But Rick wouldn't be switched. "In the other room. What signs?"

With a long sigh, she gave in and tried to explain. "You saw that scandal sheet yesterday, with that ridiculous article about Grandpa Ben and Monica Malone."

"So?"

"So, it's obvious."

"What's obvious?"

She glared at him, wondering how such a smart man could suddenly have become so dense. Still, she tried again to make him understand.

"It's just too much of a coincidence for me. All of a sudden, way too many people are interested in a man who died ten years ago. It's some reporter, Rick. Some two-bit reporter putting on an act, pulling out all the stops to get me interested enough to call her back. And I'm not going to do that."

"If it's a reporter, you can hang up on her."

"You don't know how it works. Reporters are like sharks— they have your bones picked clean before you even know what hit you. This is nothing but a scam. The woman wants more information about Grandpa Ben so that she can write more lies about him."

Rick frowned, and then his expression softened and his voice grew more gentle. "Natalie, I understand that you loved your grandfather very much. And that it must hurt you to see bad things in the press about him."

"Of course I loved him. He was a good man. A wonderful, loving man."

"I'm sure he was. But I really do believe that you're letting the hurt you feel over that trashy article about him color your judgment when it comes to this other issue."

"I am *right* about this other issue."

"If the woman's a reporter, she's a *British* reporter."

"So? Reporters come in all nationalities."

"Come on. Don't you think it's strange that she'd ask you to call her back in *London,* for heaven's sake? Wouldn't it make more sense for her to at least be here in the country if she wanted to get some big story out of you?"

"With a reporter, anything is possible."

He raised both hands, palms up. "Okay, okay. Maybe you're right. The woman could be pond scum." And then he slapped his hands down on the kitchen counter between them. He canted toward her. "But what if you're wrong?"

She took a step back, remembering, in spite of herself, the urgency in the woman's voice.

"Please. If you—or anyone you know—is a blood relative of the man, it is imperative that you get back to me."

And then she thought of her grandpa—long dead, and incapable of fighting the slanders that some heartless reporter had written about him. If she called the woman back, and let drop one tiny fact about her grandfather that she later read in some cheap tabloid newspaper, she would hate herself.

All her life, Natalie had been an easy touch. In grade school, other girls had made friends with her just for a glance at her gorgeous, famous mother or a chance to meet Kate Fortune face-to-face. And in the private high school she attended, boys had asked her out because she was a Fortune—and then invariably stammered and stared the moment they set eyes on her mother or Allie. When it came time for college, she'd gone to the University of Minnesota instead of choosing a privately funded school. There, it had gotten worse; too many of her "friends" had turned out to need money desperately—or to want an intro to one of the Fortune companies.

Still, no matter how many times she got burned, Natalie had always been ready to stick her hand in the fire one more time. But lately, she had seen too much ugliness, with all the turmoil and trouble in her family. And then there had been the humiliating way Joel Baines betrayed and then dumped her.

No, her old, trusting way of doing things just hadn't worked. It was time to stop looking at the world through the eyes of a hopeless romantic.

"I'm not wrong," she said firmly. "I know I'm not."

"But, Natalie—"

"I don't want to discuss it anymore." That came out a little harsher than she intended, but she meant it nonetheless. She reached for the bag she'd tossed on the counter. "Now, if you'll excuse me, I'm going upstairs."

She turned and started down the hall.

Rick's final words made her stop in midstride. "You cut people out without giving them a chance."

She looked at him once more, and didn't like what she saw in his eyes. She knew he was talking about more than the phone message she'd refused to return.

"I have to grow up someday," she replied flatly. "Life is not a Walt Disney movie."

After the confrontation over the phone call, Natalie found it much easier to keep her distance from Rick—because now Rick was working with her; he was doing everything in his power to stay clear of her.

She understood that she had disappointed him in some deep and important way. And it bothered her, to realize that he no longer *liked* her as much as he had before.

And yet, it was probably for the best. They had an agreement to be tenant and landlord. And no more. This way, with Rick so cool and aloof toward her, it was reasonably easy to keep that agreement whenever she dealt with him.

As the days passed, it seemed to Natalie that they fell into a sort of rhythm of avoidance. Natalie's sitting room upstairs had its own stereo, TV and VCR, so she never needed to use the parlor or the great room; they became Rick's territory.

Of course, there was only one kitchen. But they worked that out easily enough. Rick and Toby ate breakfast around seven. Natalie did her exercises and showered and came down to eat after nine. On the days that father and son didn't take the *Lady Kate* out on the lake, they were ready for lunch by eleven-thirty. Natalie ate her lunch around one. And she was careful never to try to prepare her own dinner until seven or so, by which time Rick would have long finished feeding himself and Toby.

The hardest thing for Natalie was seeing how warm and open Rick was with Toby. And with her own mother, who dropped by just about every other day. Or with Aunt Lindsay, who stopped in a couple of times on her way home from the hospital. Or even with Sterling Foster, who came by to take Natalie to lunch one afternoon. Everyone who met Rick remarked on what a great guy he was.

And they were right. Rick was terrific.

To everyone but Natalie. To Natalie, he was polite and distant and completely disengaged—until about a week after he and Toby moved in. And then he began to become hostile.

It was all so subtle at first. He mentioned tightly one afternoon that Natalie's coffee cup always seemed to be in the sink; she promised to rinse it out and put it away from now on. She left a cookbook on the counter; he reminded her coldly that she really should try to pick up after herself. She said that she would.

"I'll believe it when I see it," he said with a sneer.

And then he got all upset at her for taking his *Newsweek,* which was a perfectly understandable mistake. Hadn't she been subscribing to *Newsweek* for years? How could she have known that he subscribed, as well?

The great *Newsweek* controversy occurred on a Monday, a week and two days after Rick and Toby moved in. Rick was sitting on the porch when Natalie returned from her walk out to the mailbox. She handed him his mail. He asked for his *Newsweek.* Naturally, she told him the magazine was hers.

"Read the mailing label," he said, and not in a pleasant tone.

Natalie explained, very reasonably, that she didn't need to read the mailing label; she'd been getting *Newsweek* for years.

"There you go," he said with great disdain. "Jumping to conclusions again."

So she read the label. The magazine was his. "I'm sorry." She handed it over. "I thought—"

"I know what you thought. But you were wrong, weren't you?" And he got up from his seat and went inside, while she stood there, staring after him, feeling angry and frustrated and telling herself to just let it be.

And then, the next morning, when she was right in the middle of her step-aerobics routine, he struck again.

Natalie had just moved into the really tricky part of the routine, a series of leaps and hops from one side of the step to the other, when the pounding started on the door to her sitting room. Startled, she stumbled and turned her ankle on the step.

There was more pounding as she checked her ankle for damage and then gingerly put her weight on it. Once she'd determined that she could still walk, she armed the sweat off her forehead, hit the pause button on the VCR and marched, limping a little, to the door.

Rick was standing in the hall, a fuming look on his face and a rolled-up towel tucked under his arm. Natalie recognized the towel. Last night, she'd washed her lacy undies—the scandalously revealing ones that she'd bought for the express purpose of feeling sexy and daring. And she'd left them to dry on that towel in the laundry room.

He shoved the towel at her. "You left these in the laundry room." It was an accusation, pure and simple.

She tried for a totally nonconfrontational response. "Oh. Sorry."

He still looked positively thunderous. "Don't do it again. There's Toby to consider, in case you forgot. A five-year-old boy does not need to know about underwear like that for years yet."

She knew she should just say she'd be more careful and quietly shut the door. But he was being too ridiculous. And she was getting irritated. She asked, very quietly, "*Did* Toby see my underwear?"

He looked her up and down, and she hated him for it. She knew her hair was wet and stringy, her tank-style leotard was sweat-spotted and her ancient Nike shorts were unraveling around the leg hems. He seemed to be breathing too hard.

To be honest, she was breathing too hard, too. But she had an excuse. After all, he'd interrupted her workout.

"Did Toby see my underwear?" she asked again, when he did nothing but continue to stare at her.

He shook himself and answered curtly, "Well. No. Not that I know of."

"Good. So there's no problem. And anyway, even if he did happen to see some lacy things lying on the folding table, he'd have no idea what he was looking at."

Rick's response to that began with a grunt, an infuriatingly masculine—and superior—sound. "Some five-year-old boys have more ideas than you'd think."

"Not Toby. He's a sweetheart."

"Whether he's a sweetheart or not has nothing to do with this."

She knew he was right. And she would have gone even further: *Toby* had nothing to do with this. They were not really talking about five-year-old boys at all.

And they were both breathing too hard.

It was time to end this dangerous conversation, even at the expense of eating a little crow.

"As I said, I apologize." She felt far superior to him, because she sounded so reasonable. "I didn't think."

He made another smug grunting sound; apparently he didn't realize that she was getting the better of him by her calmness, her willingness to admit that she'd been wrong.

She gritted her teeth and spoke even more graciously. "I won't leave my lingerie down there again."

"Good," he growled, then turned without another word and marched off down the stairs.

Half an hour later, when Natalie went down for breakfast, Toby came and took her hand.

"What is it?"

Toby gave a tug. Natalie went where he pulled her, over to the coffee table in the great room, where a building-block garage had been carefully assembled.

"Did you do this by yourself?"

Toby nodded proudly.

Natalie got down on her knees and looked inside at three Matchbox cars lined up in a neat row. "Why, you have the cars in there already." She sat back on her heels. "It's really a fine garage. Great job."

Toby beamed.

Natalie didn't realize Rick was standing behind her until she pushed herself to her feet and turned. And there he was, arms folded across his broad chest, staring broodingly at her.

She blinked. "Rick? What is it?"

"Nothing."

"Are you sure?"

When he just went on staring at her, she shrugged and started to turn.

He reached out and clasped her arm.

She froze, her heart kicking into high gear, her whole body suddenly tingling. "What?"

He looked down at his own hand on her arm, and seemed bewildered as to how it had gotten there. He jerked it away. "Look. Toby and I are going out on the lake today. Do you mind if we take the dog?"

"Of course not." She wondered why he'd asked. Bernie and Toby were more or less inseparable. The dog slept every night in the child's room now, and followed the boy wherever he went. They'd been out on the boat five or six times since that first day they arrived, and Bernie had been with them every time. Rick had stopped asking if they could take the dog days ago.

"Just wanted to be sure it was all right with you." His voice was utterly flat.

"It's fine."

"Well, good." And he turned and walked away, leaving Natalie as he left her too often lately: staring after him in indignant confusion.

They were gone within the hour. Natalie should have been relieved to see Rick go, but she wasn't, not really. It was an overcast day, gray to suit her mood. The house seemed too quiet—until about ten-thirty, when Erica arrived.

Up in her rooms, Natalie heard the car screech to a stop. She ran down the stairs and pulled open the door just as her mother raised her hand to knock.

Erica's face was paler than usual. "Natalie. I'm so glad you're here."

Natalie led her mother to the kitchen, poured her some lemonade and listened to the latest distressing news about her father.

"Nathaniel called me, just an hour or so ago."

"What for?"

"He wants me to speak to Jake—and I intend to do just that."

"Why?"

"For the sake of the family."

As always, Natalie strove to provide the voice of reason. "I don't understand. I thought you said that things were really bad between you and Dad."

"They are. But Jake *is* my husband."

"But if you can't talk without fighting, how in the world are you going to get through to him 'for the sake of the family'? It makes no sense."

"I just have to see for myself that he's okay...or that he's not."

"What are you going to do if he's not?"

"I don't know. I'll deal with that problem if and when it arises."

"Look, consider the source here, all right? You know how Uncle Nate is. He never has just one reason for anything he does. He could be sending you over there because he knows what will happen."

"And what is that?"

"You and Dad will fight."

Erica waved a hand. "No, truly. Nate seemed honestly upset about Jake."

"He's always been upset about Dad."

"No, this is beyond that rivalry of theirs, more than Nathaniel being green with envy because his big brother got the head job in the family business. This was fear."

"Of what?"

"That your father really is cracking up."

"Mother, are you sure?"

"Nathaniel says that Jake shows up at the office maybe two times a week now. He's unreachable the rest of the time. Nate just called him this morning, as a matter of fact. To insist that Jake come in. Jake said he'd be there by noon, but Nate doesn't know whether to believe him or not. Nate also says that the last time Jake showed up at the office, on Friday..." Erica closed her eyes and took in a long breath.

Natalie reached for her mother's hand. "Mother?"

Erica forced herself to finish, "The last time Jake showed up at the office, he was drunk."

It took Natalie a moment to digest that piece of information. It seemed so completely out of character for her father. Jacob Fortune was a powerful, self-possessed man. He would never allow himself to appear at his office under the influence of anything but his own indomitable will.

Erica drew up her shoulders. "Nat, I'm going over there." Then she turned pleading eyes on her daughter.

Natalie sighed; she knew what was coming.

"And if I go alone, you've already predicted what will happen—an argument. Probably a very bad one."

"You want me to go with you." It wasn't a question.

"Oh, Nat. If you would. Please."

"Mother..."

"Please?"

Natalie reminded herself, as she was always doing, that she was not going to be drawn into the family drama. Never again. No way.

Still, if even Uncle Nate was worried about her father, things must be bad.

"Nat, will you?"

Natalie swallowed. "Now?"

Erica leaned forward and brushed a strand of hair back from Natalie's cheek, the way she used to do all the time, years ago, when Natalie was little. "Yes, let's go now. I just...I feel so agitated. I don't think I'll be able to settle down at all until I've seen him. Until I talk to him and find out exactly how bad this really is."

Natalie was weakening. How could she help it? The need in her mother's eyes was so strong. "Shouldn't we call first? What if he's not there?"

"If we call, he might say he won't see us. And if he's

not there... Well, it's only a wasted trip around the lake. Let's just go now. Please.''

"Mother—"

"*Please.*"

Natalie knew she was beaten. "All right. Let's go.''

Nine

Though they could have used the ski boat that was waiting in the boathouse, Erica wanted to drive. So they took the long way around the lake, through the forest of elm and maple and oak that was so green and lush that time of year.

By the time they reached the estate's front entrance, a steady, soft rain had begun to fall. They rang the bell. A female voice Natalie didn't recognize answered. "Yes, who is it, please?"

"Erica and Natalie to see Jake," her mother said.

"Please wait."

A few minutes later, the voice told them to drive right in. The big iron gates swung wide and then closed behind them automatically.

It wasn't long before they were turning into the sweeping drive before the colonnaded front of the main house. Everything looked just as Natalie remembered it. Beneath the misty veil of the rain, the lawns were the same deep swaths of emerald and the ornamental shrubs were trimmed and neat. Whatever was going on with Natalie's father, at least the groundskeepers were still doing their job.

Jake's head driver appeared just as Erica pulled the Mercedes to a stop. He opened her door for her, holding a large black umbrella so that she wouldn't get wet.

"How are you, Edgar?" Erica emerged from the car and into the shelter of Edgar's umbrella.

"Just fine, ma'am."

Erica handed him the keys. "Don't take it far." She and Edgar began walking toward the wide front steps, the driver scrupulously careful not to let Erica get wet. "I have no idea how long we'll be, but probably not too long."

"Yes, ma'am."

Natalie was already out of the car and dashing across the polished flagstones toward the marble steps when Edgar turned to assist her as he had her mother. He looked at her reproachfully as she flew past him between the tall columns, into the shelter of the portico.

She grinned at him. "Good to see you, Edgar."

"Yes, miss." He held the umbrella over his own head now. His tone, as always, was terribly proper and reserved. "It's good to see you, too."

Natalie hurried to join her mother, who had already turned and approached the massive front door. Almost before Erica finished ringing the bell, the door was pulled back by a gray-haired woman in a plain blue skirt and blouse.

"Hello, Mrs. Fortune." It was the same voice they'd heard over the intercom.

"Hello. I don't believe I know you."

"I'm Mrs. Laughlin, the new housekeeper."

"I see. I'd like to speak with my husband, please."

"Certainly. Mr. Fortune asked me to bring you to the library." The woman closed the big door. "This way." She started to turn.

"I know the way to the library," Erica said.

The housekeeper stopped where she was. "You mean you...don't wish to be announced?"

"No. I can announce myself. Very effectively."

Natalie cast a quick glance at her mother. Erica's elegant shoulders were high and proud, her chin was tilted defiantly, her famous cheekbones were flushed a deep rose. The nervous, needy woman who'd arrived at Natalie's house half an hour before might never have existed. Erica was anticipating the battle with the primary adversary—and grand passion—of her life: her husband.

"You may return to your duties," Erica told Mrs. Laughlin.

The housekeeper had clearly been given firm orders to escort them to the library. "But..." Her protest faded when she met Erica's determined gaze. "As you wish." With a slight nod of acquiescence, she retreated, her crepe-soled shoes whispering on the polished floor.

When she was gone, Erica turned to Natalie. "How long has she been here?"

Natalie shrugged. "I've never seen her before."

Erica raised a hand to her neck. The emerald that Jake had given her years ago sent out glints of green fire in the dim entry hall. "If the staff is quitting—"

"Mother. Let's not jump to conclusions, all right? The fact that Dad's hired a new housekeeper doesn't necessarily mean anything."

"You're right, of course. Sorry."

"Let's just go see Dad, all right?"

"Yes. Let's go."

Side by side, mother and daughter walked down the huge central hall to the library's massive double doors. When they reached them, Erica drew in a deep breath, took one polished brass handle in each slender fist and pulled the doors wide.

Inside the library, Jacob Fortune sat in the high-backed swivel chair behind the sprawling leather-topped desk that had dominated the room for as long as Natalie could remember. He was wearing one of his beautiful Armani suits. His proud shoulders were drawn back, his lean hands before him on the desk. He looked up sharply when the doors opened, and his dark eyes narrowed at the sight of his wife.

"Hello....darling." Erica paused just long enough before the endearment that it almost sounded like a curse.

"Erica." There were a thousand shades of meaning in the single word. In it, Natalie could hear love and hate, despair—and tenderness.

For an extended moment, husband and wife stared at each other. Watching them, Natalie felt totally irrelevant. Oh, what in the world had possessed her to let her mother talk her into this? She shouldn't be here. Erica Fortune was perfectly capable of fighting her own battles with Jake; she'd been doing it for years, after all.

And, oddly, at the same time she longed to be elsewhere, Natalie couldn't help thinking of Rick. Because the way her father looked at her mother seemed, at that moment, to be exactly the way Rick looked at *her* lately.

Which was ridiculous. There was no grand, ruined passion between herself and Rick Dalton. She was Natalie, after all, the ordinary one, not the type to inspire any overwhelming emotions. Men liked her. They got comfortable with her. They depended on her. And, too often, they took advantage of her. But they certainly didn't look at her as if she'd single-handedly crushed all their dreams.

"Don't stand on ceremony. Just walk right in." Jake laid on the irony when at last he spoke again.

"Thank you. I will." Erica swept into the room, Natalie in her wake.

"Hello, Nat." Her father's voice was warm. Though

there had been conflicts between her father and more than
one of her other siblings, Jake and Natalie had always
gotten along. Natalie, after all, was neither brilliant nor
beautiful. Nor was she a son. She served no purpose
whatsoever in Jake's dreams of empire. Thus, he could
love her unconditionally and leave her to make her own
choices in life.

She gave him an uncomfortable smile. "Dad."

Jake's look became scathing once more as he turned
it on his wife. "Whatever you're up to, you shouldn't
have dragged poor Nat into it."

Erica's perfect chin remained lifted high. "I needed
support."

Jake made a low scoffing noise, then stood and came
around the desk. He gestured at a brocade sofa nearby.
"Have a seat." Natalie started for the sofa, but her mother's voice stopped her.

"Thank you, no. We can't stay but a moment." Erica
frowned as she looked Jake up and down. "You
look...well enough."

And he did, Natalie thought. Not *well*, exactly: there
were dark circles beneath his eyes and the grooves
around his mouth were much deeper than Natalie remembered. No, he didn't look *well*. But he did look *well
enough.*

Jake raised a silvered brow. "So. You're here to check
up on me."

Erica didn't flinch. "That's exactly why I'm here."

"What led you to believe I needed checking on?"

"Nathaniel."

Jake took in a long breath. "Dear brother Nate.
Scheming as usual." He spread his arms and looked
down at his body—at his impeccable jacket, his perfectly

creased trousers and his polished, glove-soft shoes. "Well, as you can see, I'm getting along just fine."

Erica shook her head. "Jake. I do read the papers."

He dropped his hands and gave his wife a stare that would have had a lesser woman shaking in her Norma Kamali shoes. "Don't presume to understand the choices I make for Fortune Industries."

Erica smiled then, a smile so cold it sent a chill through Natalie. "No, Jake. Don't worry. I won't presume to understand anything about you. Ever again." She turned to Natalie. "I think it's time we were going. It's obvious that coming here was a complete waste of time."

"Oh, and your time is so damn precious, isn't it, Erica?" Though Jake spoke the words under his breath, they were perfectly clear.

Erica gasped. Natalie shot a glance at her mother and cringed at the stricken look on her face.

Aside from her modeling career, which was long behind her now, Jake had always insisted that Erica dedicate her life to him and the raising of their family. For him to taunt her now because she had no important work to do was dirty fighting in the extreme.

And Erica clearly wasn't going to take the blow without retaliating. She whirled on her husband, her eyes bright with wounded fury. "Why, you—"

But before she could say one more outraged word, Natalie stepped forward and took her arm. "Mother. Don't."

Erica froze and shot Natalie a quick, reproachful glance.

Jake spoke again. "Yes. She's right. I shouldn't have said that."

Still Erica said nothing, only glared at her husband.

"I...apologize," Jake said.

It was a major concession from a man like Jake. Beside her, Natalie felt her mother relax just a little.

Erica nodded. "Very well." The fire in her eyes had turned to ice. "We'll be going, then, as I said."

For a moment, Jake just stared at his wife. Then his glance slid away. "Yes. I think that's for the best."

But Erica didn't move.

So Natalie gave a small tug. "Mother, let's go."

It was enough. Erica went with her, through the doors that remained open onto the hall.

Once they'd left, Jake waited, standing absolutely still, until he was sure they wouldn't return. Then he strode to the double doors and pulled them shut.

After that, assured of privacy, he headed straight for the liquor cabinet—and the crystal decanter he sought. He poured himself a generous three fingers of Scotch and knocked it back in two throat-burning swallows.

His second drink he took more slowly. By the time he had it down, the knot in his gut had eased a little.

There was nothing to worry about. He had handled himself well enough. Erica and Natalie had left thinking he was okay. Nate might have sent them here hoping to put more pressure on him, but he'd fooled brother Nate.

Jake caught a glimpse of himself in one of the beveled glass panes of the liquor cabinet doors, and quickly turned away. He didn't like what he saw when he looked into his own eyes lately. He didn't like it one damn bit. Sometimes he wondered who the hell he was, anyway. Because, as that blackmailing bitch Monica Malone had so gleefully pointed out to him, he was not who everyone thought he was.

With a low growl that sounded like a noise a trapped animal might make, Jake returned to the desk, where he dropped into the big chair and stared broodingly at the carved double doors that led out onto the empty hall.

Monica.

He couldn't get her off his mind.

Sometimes he wondered whether everything—*everything* that was pulling his family and his world apart—began and ended with her. The fires at the labs. Kate's death. Allie's stalker. All of it. Every damn insurmountable difficulty, caused by Monica Malone.

Lately, the scandal sheets had been full of stories of how she had loved Ben Fortune. Was that it? Thwarted love, turned bitter and murderous over the years?

If she had loved Ben, that would explain a lot. Lovers whispered things to each other, after all. They revealed secrets they'd be wiser to keep to themselves.

And Monica Malone knew plenty of secrets. The bitch had an inside track on too much. She knew things she had no damn right to know. Like the fact that Jake was not really Ben Fortune's son...

Damn. What sick pleasure she'd taken in telling him all about it. In pointing out that he'd been born just six months after Ben and Kate's wedding—and such a *big* baby, too. She'd described how his real father, some nobody G.I. named Joe Stover, had died on a battlefield in France before Jake was even born. How Ben had been so in love with Kate that he promised to raise her bastard as his own.

Oh, and Ben had kept his promise. Jake had never been told about the man who'd really fathered him. He'd been treated as Ben's oldest son in all the ways that mattered—even if deep in his heart he'd sometimes felt that he didn't really completely belong. Still, the lie had been passed on to the next generation. Jake's children had grown up adoring their wonderful grandpa Ben.

Ben and Kate had gone to their graves with the secret. It was never to have been revealed.

But somehow, Monica Malone had known. And six months ago, she'd made sure that Jake knew, as well. And now she was bleeding him and his company dry as the price for not revealing the truth to the world.

Yanking his tie loose, Jake leaned back with a sigh. The cut-crystal glass he still held in his hand was empty.

He wanted another.

But he wouldn't have one. He would get to the damn office by noon and show his back-stabbing half brother that he could still hold it together. Whatever new trick Monica Malone had up her silken sleeve, he would deal with it. He ran Fortune Industries, and that wasn't going to change.

He'd given up his own dreams years ago to follow in Ben Fortune's footsteps. He wasn't going to hand over his position now; it was all he had left, after all.

He closed his eyes. For a moment, on the dark inside of his lids, he saw Erica. Erica smiling, reaching out her soft arms to him, as she used to do, before all the garbage between them got in the way.

And then her silvery image faded—to be replaced by Monica Malone, grinning that evil come-hither grin of hers. The woman was capable of anything. Anything.

Before she started blackmailing him, she'd actually tried to seduce him. God. She had to be in her sixties. A decade older than he was, at the very least. But still beautiful. Beautiful, and hard as nails. They didn't make them meaner—or craftier—than Monica Malone.

Low and crudely, Jake swore. Something was going to have to be done about her. Very soon.

His fingers tightened on his empty glass.

One more. Just one more. And then he'd call for the car and be on his way.

Erica didn't stay long after she and Natalie arrived back at the farmhouse. She kissed her daughter and thanked her for going with her to see that Jake was all right.

"I couldn't have done it without you."

"Yes, Mom. You could have."

"Not without saying things I would have regretted."

Natalie didn't argue that point. "Well, it's done now."

"Yes. And I do feel a little better, knowing Jake's not all that bad off. I promise you, the way Nathaniel talked, I really thought he was becoming an alcoholic, or worse." She laughed her brittle laugh. "Ridiculous, isn't it?"

Natalie agreed that it was. Since the rain had cleared off by then, she stood by the front walk, watching as her mother drove away much more sedately than she had arrived, not fishtailing once or throwing up any gravel at all.

Then she turned and went into the house, which was empty; Toby, Bernie and Rick wouldn't return for hours yet.

Natalie tried to sit down with a book on innovative teaching techniques that she'd been meaning to read, but she couldn't concentrate. She felt edgy.

Maybe it was uneasiness about her father.

Though she hadn't wanted to worry her mother, Natalie wasn't at all sure that Jake was okay. His eyes had looked so haunted. And in hindsight it seemed that his self-assurance and cool control had been more an act than the real thing. As if he had been somehow playing the part of himself. Going through the motions of being the Jake Fortune his wife and daughter had always known.

"Ridiculous." Though there was no one there to hear, Natalie used the same word her mother had used.

She'd be wise to stop thinking about her father, unless she intended to try to find out what was bothering him—which would put her, once again, right in the middle of all the family turmoil she kept telling herself she wanted to escape. And which Jake wouldn't appreciate at all. One of his and Erica's problems had always been that he wouldn't share his feelings with his wife. And if he wouldn't share them with Erica, then he certainly wouldn't reveal them to Natalie.

No, Natalie told herself. There was nothing she could do about whatever was disturbing her father. She just had to stop worrying.

In the great room, she stood at the bank of windows and stared out at the lake, wistfully wondering how late it would be before the *Lady Kate* came back—and then despising herself when she realized what she was doing.

She reminded herself of her last two encounters with Rick. Early this morning when he'd come pounding on her door to yell at her about her underwear. And then, after that, when he'd managed to make asking whether he could take Bernie out on the boat into a hostile encounter. She truly was a doormat *extraordinaire*, to be longing for the return of a man who shot her surly looks when she passed him in the hall and only spoke to her to tell her what she was doing wrong.

Maybe she really should move out. Not across the lake. No, after today, she could see that would be a big mistake. She could stay at her mother's—but even the · thought of that had her shaking her head. Lindsay and

Frank would welcome her. But they had such a busy life; she'd feel she was in the way.

A hotel would probably be the best choice. And she wouldn't have to live there for long. It was less than a week until her departure—which, really, was hardly any time at all. She turned from the window and saw Toby's garage made of blocks, on the coffee table. She smiled a melancholy smile. She would miss Toby. A lot.

And, to be fair, most of the time she and Rick managed well enough. The house was big. If she only made an effort to avoid him for a few more days, everything would work out all right.

She'd be off to see the world. And when she returned, Rick and his darling little boy would go back to Minneapolis where they belonged.

Resolutely she marched over to the phone and called up a friend who lived in Travistown. They made a date for that night. An early dinner at the local inn. Natalie would be out of the house before Rick, the boy and the dog came in from the lake.

At about the same time Natalie was making plans, Sterling visited Kate in her Minneapolis apartment.

"We've found the leak on the tabloid story about Ben and Monica Malone," Sterling said.

"Who was it?"

"The Malone woman herself. Gabe was able to have a little talk with a certain day maid that Ms. Malone just fired."

"And?"

"The maid named the reporter and the date she visited Monica's mansion, which was two days before the story appeared. Evidently, all Monica asked was that she not be named as the source."

Kate sat perfectly still as the news sank in. Then she said very softly, "If there was ever any doubt, there's none now. She's out to destroy us."

Sterling said nothing.

Kate thought about Jake. Ben had promised to raise her oldest child as his own. And he had. He'd done well by Jake. No one had ever known that Jake wasn't his son.

But if Ben had betrayed his wedding vows, what else might he have been capable of? It cut Kate to the heart to think it, but could Ben have committed the ultimate indiscretion? During some moment of forbidden intimacy, had he whispered the truth about Jake's parentage to Monica Malone?

And was Monica now using what she knew to get Jake to dance to her tune?

"Something has to be done about her," Kate said.

"Yes," Sterling agreed. "The question is, what?"

The doors were locked when Rick, Toby and the dog came in from the lake.

Toby looked up at Rick, and Rick read the question in his eyes.

"Looks like she's not home." He dug the key from his pocket and opened the door. Toby, who reeked of the panfish he liked to catch and then throw back in the lake, slipped in ahead of him. "Bath first, then dinner," Rick instructed, before the boy could escape to his room.

Toby stopped, turned and looked at his father. His glance said both *Okay* and *I know what to do, Dad.* Then he and the dog headed off down the hall.

Rick carried the cooler into the kitchen and unloaded it. Then he found the remote and turned on the set in the great room, planning to keep an eye on the news while he was fixing dinner.

He was switching channels, looking for some national news, when he landed on a station that was airing "Hot Copy," a syndicated pseudonews show. The current sound bite concerned the Fortunes. Rick paused with his finger on the button that would change the channel and listened to another quick recap of all the things he'd already heard—from continued speculation about the relationship between Ben Fortune and the ageless Monica Malone to all the questions surrounding the new Fortune heiress, Tracey Ducet.

There was a brief interview with the Ducet woman, who really did look a hell of a lot like Natalie's aunt Lindsay. "I'm hopin' that, as time goes by, the family will learn to accept me," Tracey drawled. And Rick almost felt sorry for her. If she *was* a fake, she was a very appealing one. She had a nice, shy smile, and somehow the corn-pone accent and the bad clothes made her more sympathetic—a poor, lost little girl trying to play games way out of her league.

Next, there was a brief mention of the rumored rift between the older generation of Fortune sons, Jacob and Nathaniel, and then a description of the current upheavals within the Fortune companies. A photographic montage of the Fortune family history ended the story, starting with pictures of Kate and Ben as newlyweds during the war, and concluding with aerial shots of the demolished plane in which Kate Fortune had lost her life. There was actually a shot of Natalie, as a little girl, in a red velvet dress with a white lace collar, posed along with all the other Fortunes around a giant Christmas tree. Her name wasn't mentioned, but Rick would have known those big, soft brown eyes anywhere.

A commercial came on. Rick switched the channel. But then, instead of getting up, he stayed crouched in front of the big set, staring blankly at the screen and thinking about Natalie.

He felt guilty about his behavior that morning. The way he pounded on her door and read her the riot act had been more than a little out of line.

The problem was, she was driving him crazy. He'd been thinking about her and telling himself not to when he went into the laundry room, headed for the pantry closet to get another box of the Super Wheat Crunchies Toby liked. He'd seen those little scraps of silk and lace spread out there on that damn towel.

The first thing that had come to mind was what she might look like wearing such things. His mouth had gone dry and his jeans had gotten too tight. And then he'd had to wonder what lucky S.O.B. had seen her like that. And at that point, something inside him had snapped. He'd rolled the things in the towel and marched up the stairs to tell her just what he thought of her leaving her underwear around for anyone to see.

When she opened the door and stood there, all shiny and sweaty in her clingy leotard and little blue shorts with the stripes on the sides, he'd wanted to grab her, pull her up hard against the part of him that seemed to ache all the time lately and bring his mouth down hard on hers.

Of course, he couldn't do that. She'd drawn the line on stuff like that.

So he'd told her off instead.

And then later, when she came downstairs to get her breakfast and Toby beckoned her over to admire his building-block garage, he hadn't been able to keep himself from watching her. From watching the way she was with Toby, so sweet and tender and good. As he'd noticed that first moment he set eyes on her in her silly spangles and ridiculous platform shoes, she looked damned enticing from behind.

She'd turned around before he could look away, and caught him gawking at her like some kind of lovesick teenager. At least she hadn't looked down. If she had, she would have seen the effect she had on him. As it was, he didn't think she'd noticed. Still, he'd felt like a fool. So he'd made a big deal out of asking her whether he could take the dog out on the lake, even though they'd tacitly agreed early on that the dog was more or less Toby's for the summer.

He should be nicer to her. He knew that. She was a nice woman. And, apparently, the old boyfriend had hurt her pretty bad. He had no right to blame her for not wanting to get involved with another man right now.

He had no right—but he did. Because he wanted her. And it was a wanting that seemed to get stronger with every day that passed.

He wasn't dealing with it well.

Just as he hadn't dealt well with his marriage to Vanessa.

He'd messed up with Vanessa, he knew that. She'd been beautiful and spoiled. And used to having what she wanted. She'd made it clear from that first night he met her that she wanted *him*. He'd just started at Langley, Bates and Shears. A kid from a working-class background, ready to design shopping malls and steel-and-glass offices for a white-collar world.

Vanessa had been from a good family. She'd been raised in a nice neighborhood in Louisville by a mother who involved herself in community affairs. Her father, deceased when Rick met her, had owned a small chain of drugstores. Rick had married her because he thought she'd make the kind of wife he needed.

Oh, yeah, he'd called it love, and he'd been totally infatuated at first. But had it really been love? He couldn't be certain anymore.

It had gone to pieces quickly. Vanessa had wanted more attention than he could afford to give her. She'd gotten pregnant sooner than either of them planned—and then hated him for making her that way. By the time Toby was born, they'd hardly been speaking. And then, when Toby was barely a year old, she'd taken him and walked out, returning to the one person who knew how to love her and lavish on her the attention she craved— her mother.

Rick had immersed himself in work. He'd sent the alimony and support checks before they were due.

And for the next four years, he hadn't allowed a woman to get to him in any way that mattered. If a woman came on to him, he made it clear up front that he was single and planning to stay that way. They took him on those terms, for as long as it lasted, or they walked away right at the start. He'd seen no reason at all to let himself want them too much.

But then there had been the accident. And Toby had come back to him. And his whole life had been upended, turned inside out. And he'd seen how damn empty it was.

And then, not quite a month ago, he'd walked into this house and seen Natalie. And almost immediately, he'd started wanting her. The sound of her laughter sent his nerves humming. The sight of her coffee cup in the sink destroyed him. He couldn't forget the way she smiled at Toby, the way she scratched Bernie behind the ears. Her scent seemed to linger on the air, whether she was in the house or not. And a glimpse of her, out on the front lawn, wearing old cutoffs, with her hair pulled back in a sloppy ponytail, could arouse him more thoroughly than any skilled lover he'd ever known.

But it was bad timing. The moment he laid eyes on her, he'd started to see that he was ready, at last, to take a chance again—while she wasn't.

And, in retrospect, he had to admit to himself that he should have been more understanding about that phone call from the Englishwoman. He still didn't believe that the woman was a fraud. But he hadn't lived Natalie's life. He wasn't from a prominent family. He had no idea what it might be like to have people pretend to be what they weren't for the sake of a newspaper story.

He had to be nicer to her. He *would* be nicer to her. He would not hold it against her that she refused to give him what he really wanted from her. It was her choice. And, damn it, he would show her that he was capable of respecting a woman's choice.

Ten

Natalie pulled up to the house at a little before nine. The lights in the front parlor were on. Rick was probably in there. Since she wanted to stay clear of him, she parked her car in the garage, let herself in through the back door and headed straight for the central hall and the stairs.

She had her hand on the newel post and her foot on the first riser when Rick's voice stopped her.

"Natalie..." He was standing in the door to the parlor, wearing a gray sweatshirt, old jeans and a pair of moccasins. The shirt was soft and clung to the strong, broad shape of his shoulders.

So much for escape. She stopped and looked at him.

"Hi," he said. He was smiling.

She wondered whether she was seeing things. He hadn't smiled at her in days. Her heart beat faster, for which she despised it.

"Hi," she said, and waited.

But he didn't seem to have anything more to say.

So she said, "Good night," and started up the stairs again.

He coughed. "Natalie, I..."

She stopped on the second step and waited some more. Still he didn't go on. So she asked in a wary tone, "Yes?"

He folded his arms over his chest, shifted from one

moccasin to the other. "I wonder if we could talk. Just for a minute or two."

The way he'd been behaving lately, she probably wouldn't like what he had to say. But to refuse might only make him mad, and she was trying to keep things on an even keel with him. So she murmured grudgingly, "All right."

His smile became rueful. He turned a little and gestured toward the sofa in the room behind him. "Come in here, why don't you? Sit down."

She frowned. They *were* supposed be avoiding each other. And he really had been mean lately. She didn't know quite how to take him now.

He went on smiling in that thoroughly charming, rueful way. "Please. I won't bite. I promise."

That made her laugh a little, but it was a nervous sound. He gestured toward the couch again. So she came across the threshold and went past him, to sit where he had indicated.

He followed a moment later, dropping into a wing chair opposite her. Once there, he seemed not to know how to begin. He rested his elbows on the chair arms, folded his hands on his stomach and then looked down at his hands, as if studying them.

Natalie found herself staring at his hands, too. They were well-shaped hands, with long fingers and neatly trimmed nails. Very handsome hands, actually.

"Look. I've been thinking about a few things."

"Yes?" She sounded ridiculously hopeful. And she was sitting forward, leaning toward him. She made herself sit back, and counted to five before she spoke again. "What things?"

"I know I've been...hard on you lately."

Suddenly there was a pressure at the back of her throat and she found it difficult to look at him.

"Natalie?"

She made herself lift her chin and face him. "Yes. You certainly have. Been hard on me, I mean."

He shifted around in the chair. "I...judged you harshly, when you wouldn't call that Holmes woman back."

"That's right, you did."

"And I've been out of line about some other things lately. I went overboard about the *Newsweek*. And I overreacted about your..." He cast about for a suitable word for her underwear.

She provided it. "Lingerie."

He coughed. "Right. I guess the real deal here is that I want a chance with you and you're not giving me one. And I'm..."

"Sulking?"

He grunted. "Men don't sulk."

Wisely, she refrained from argument on that point.

"I...apologize."

Lord. He sounded just the way her father had sounded apologizing to Erica this morning. Like Jake, Rick was making saying he was sorry into a major concession. Natalie experienced a sudden flash of irritation at all men.

Rick must have seen her exasperation in her eyes. "What? You don't accept my apology?" Now he sounded noble. And slightly wounded.

She longed to say something snappish and hurtful, to get back at him a little for the way he'd been treating her. But what good would that do, really? She lifted her chin and squared her shoulders. "No. I do. I accept your apology."

He made a sound of disbelief, which reminded her of

her father, too. And suddenly she felt very tired. She looked away, toward the dark windows.

The room was quiet. Then Rick said, "What is it?"

She turned to him. "What do you mean?"

"Something's bothering you." He granted her that rueful smile again. "Other than me, I mean."

For some totally incomprehensible reason, she found that she wanted to tell him. Everything. About her father and her mother and the odd, scary way her father had been behaving. She wanted to *confide* in him, of all things. To confide in a *man*.

She remembered the day he and Toby had arrived to stay. She'd confided in Rick that day, out on the lake, told him too much about her childhood and her sisters, about Joel and their breakup. It hadn't been like her at all. Natalie Fortune did not confide in men. Men confided in *her*.

"Natalie. Tell me."

"Oh, Rick..."

"Come on." His blue gaze was so tender, so full of honest concern. He really did seem to want to know.

But her family's never-ending difficulties had nothing to do with him. She shook her head.

Rick stared at her intently for a moment more. "All right. Whatever." He glanced down at his hands again, then back at her. "Look. It's only a few days now until you leave."

"Five days."

"Yes. And during that time, I want us to be..." He sought the right word.

She tried to help him. "Friends?"

He winced. "God. Talk about clichés."

"How about 'on friendly terms,' then."

He considered, then nodded. "That's better." His eyes narrowed. "You look doubtful."

"I guess I am, a little."

"Why?"

"Well, even though I'm the one who suggested it, I can't help wondering what being 'on friendly terms' is going to entail."

"Nothing much. I promise."

She looked at him sideways.

He chuckled. "Now you're wondering what exactly I mean by 'nothing much.'"

"Yes. I suppose I am."

"I mean, we'll just…make an effort to get along, that's all. I *don't* mean we have to share meals or go out on the *Lady Kate* together."

She felt disappointed—and detested herself for it.

He continued, "But we could…exchange a few pleasant words now and then, when we pass in the hall. Even share a little conversation when we happen to be in the same room together." He was watching her closely. "So. What do you think?"

It sounded lovely. She didn't like living in this hostile silence they shared now. And yet it seemed dangerous, to let down her guard with him. She really was drawn to him. And he was so frank about being attracted to her.

Could this be some kind of trick on his part?

But that was ridiculous. She was being paranoid.

Next she'd be thinking he was after her because she was a Fortune and he wanted to get his hands on her money, or make use of her connections.

"Damn it, Natalie. I *like* you."

She believed him. But she knew she shouldn't. Hadn't she proved conclusively that her judgment was truly awful when it came to men?

Rick rubbed one of those good-looking hands down his equally good-looking face.

And that was another thing: Rick was much better-looking than any man she'd ever gone out with. It wasn't just physical, though his body was big and well proportioned and his features were arranged compellingly. It was something in his eyes. And in the way he carried himself. Something strong and determined.

Something totally male.

The few men she'd dated had been a lot like Joel, in all honesty. Just a little bit less than all man. Just a little bit weak.

Rick Dalton was not weak.

He was frowning again, as he tried his very best to be patient. But she'd taken way too long to answer him, and he was clearly worrying about what might be going through her mind.

She stood. "I like you, too, Rick."

He looked up at her, and his fine mouth twitched at the corners. "Thank God for small favors."

"And I'd like to be...friendly. Until I leave."

The next morning, when Natalie came downstairs, Rick smiled at her and told her the coffee was hot. She poured herself a cup and sat down in the padded rocker in the great room with Toby, who was watching cartoons and building some kind of spaceport out of a plastic construction set. With Bernie sprawled close by, she rocked and watched Toby and sipped her coffee, while Rick sat at the breakfast table reading the *Star Tribune.*

Eventually she got up and poached herself an egg and sat down across from Rick to eat. Once or twice, when he was turning the pages of his paper, Rick spoke to her—casual things. He told her teasingly that Dayton's was having a big sale starting Friday.

"Now *that* you won't want to miss."

She pretended to yawn. "I'll mark it on my calendar."

He chuckled. "You might get yourself a deal on platform shoes."

She knew he was referring to that very first day, when he'd caught her singing along with Bernie and Janis, all dressed up in bangles and beads. She played along with his teasing. "What about lampshades?"

"That's right. I guess you probably get tired of wearing the same one all the time."

She agreed that she did.

He told her that lamps and lamp shades were going to be half-off.

"That does it. I'll be there," she vowed.

They talked about the Twins—who were not having the best of years. Rick said he preferred the Saints, anyway. And they played at the St. Paul Municipal Stadium, which was out-of-doors, unlike the Twins, who played their home games at the Metrodome.

"Baseball should be played outside," he said.

She was with him on that. "And the minor-league games are more fun, anyway. It always feels more like they're playing the game for love."

"A guy in the minors has to love it," Rick said. "If he didn't, he'd find something that paid better."

Natalie happened to glance over, and saw that Toby was watching them. Maybe she was taking this "friendliness" thing a little too far.

She stood and carried her dirty dishes to the sink. As she rinsed them and put them in the dishwasher, she caught herself humming a tune from *Pocahontas*. She stopped that foolishness right away. And when she glanced at Rick, he was hidden behind his paper. Obviously, he hadn't heard. And even if he *had* heard, it didn't matter. It was only a silly song.

That evening, Natalie played Concentration with Toby. Together they spread the deck of cards facedown on the rug in the great room. Then they took turns trying to choose pairs. Toby was surprisingly good at it. He matched several pairs after seeing a mate only once.

After Toby was in bed, it just seemed natural that Natalie and Rick would sit in the great room and talk for a while. They didn't talk about anything in particular, really. There were some loose boards out in the boathouse, Rick said. She thanked him for telling her and told him she'd get someone over from the estate to handle the repair. He was taking Toby into the Cities tomorrow. Was there anything he could pick up for her? She said she was going in herself. Bernie had a date at the dog groomer's for his final bath and comb-out before she left on her trip. She almost suggested that they all just go together.

But she stopped herself. After all, they'd agreed that they weren't going to take this thing too far.

The next night, Erica called just as Rick was tucking Toby in. Natalie's mother was fretting over Jake again, having second thoughts very similar to Natalie's about their visit to the estate.

"The more I think about it, the more strange the whole encounter seemed. Do you know what I mean, Nat?"

Natalie didn't want to lie, but she didn't want to add to her mother's worries, either. So she made a noncommittal noise.

Erica went on, "His hair was wet, did you notice? As if he'd just showered. But it was after eleven. That's the scariest thing, when I really let myself think about it. That he was there, at the estate, and not at the office. After eleven on a weekday. That's not the Jake I know at all. And his eyes. His eyes looked wrong, Nat. Terribly troubled. Did you notice?''

Natalie did her best to soothe her mother, reminding her that even if there was something really bothering Jake, no one could help him if he didn't want to be helped.

"And hasn't that always been the problem with Jacob?'' Erica said sadly. "He keeps it all in. It's almost impossible to know what's really going on inside him.''

"I'm sure he'll be fine.'' Natalie tried her best to believe her own words.

A few minutes later, her mother said goodbye. Natalie hung up just as Rick returned from Toby's room.

One look at her face and he was demanding, "Who was that on the phone?''

"Just my mother.''

"What did she say that's got you upset?''

The other night, she'd put him off. But right then, the offer of a friendly ear was just too tempting.

Five minutes later, they were sitting at either end of the sofa in the great room and Natalie was sharing her concern about her father.

Rick listened and agreed that it didn't sound good. "But I don't know what you can do about it.''

"I don't really think there's anything. Except to be available if he needs me. And to try to stop worrying about him.'' She gathered her legs up to the side and leaned a little closer to Rick. "Thanks for listening. I feel better, just having someone to tell it to.''

"Any time.''

They shared a long look. Natalie was feeling so

warmly toward him. She really loved the way they were getting along now.

All at once, Rick cut his eyes away. He stood. "I think I'll go out on the back porch. Listen to the cicadas."

She was a little surprised at his abruptness, but she covered it up with teasing. "And get eaten alive by the mosquitoes?"

His chuckle sounded slightly forced. "Why not?"

He hadn't invited her to accompany him, and she assumed he must want to be alone. So she stayed where she was as he went out the back door.

She'd rented a movie, a romantic comedy, from the store in Travistown. It was waiting on top of the VCR in her sitting room upstairs.

Maybe Rick would enjoy watching it with her.

She went up and got it. When she came back down, he was still out on the porch. She started for the back door.

And then nervousness assailed her. Maybe he really didn't want to be bothered right now. Maybe—

She was being a fool. She knew it. Making a big deal over a simple little thing like asking him if he'd like to share a movie with her.

She decided she'd make popcorn first. That would give him a few more minutes outside, undisturbed, and provide her with something to do while she built up her nerve. She marched over and plunked the tape down on top of the television, then proceeded to the kitchen, where she got out a bag of microwave popcorn.

In minutes, it was ready. She poured the fat, butter-flavored kernels into a bowl and carried the bowl into the great room, where she set it on the coffee table next to Toby's latest project: a Matchbox car kit called Emergency City.

Rick came back in just as she was telling herself she couldn't put off extending her invitation a moment more.

"What's this? Popcorn?"

Her tongue was suddenly too big inside her mouth. "Yes, um, I rented a movie. A comedy. I thought maybe..."

"Sounds great. Want a soda?"

"A soda. Yes. Great."

So Rick got two colas and Natalie slipped the video into the VCR in the cabinet under the television. They sat on the floor by the coffee table and munched their popcorn, sipped their sodas and watched the movie. Natalie tried not to think about how they laughed at all the same places. And she was careful not to glance at Rick when the guy in the movie finally kissed the girl. And when she and Rick both reached into the bowl at the same time, and his hand brushed hers, she scrupulously ignored the delicious little shiver that skittered up her arm.

As soon as the movie was through, Natalie put the popcorn bowl in the dishwasher, tossed her empty cola can in the recycling bin and told Rick good-night.

The next morning, she woke smiling, thinking of Rick. She told herself *that* had to stop. She'd be more careful today, she decided; she'd keep a little more distance between them.

But when she came downstairs and saw him at the table, reading his paper, it just seemed the most natural thing in the world to pour herself some coffee and sit down opposite him, to hear about what he was reading in the paper and answer his questions about the itinerary for her Mediterranean cruise.

And, actually, time was running very short for the two of them, anyway. Their days together in the house were almost over. It was Friday. On Monday, early, she would fly to New York. From New York she'd board a plane for Tenerife, her ship's embarkation point.

Really, going out of her way to avoid Rick was unnecessary. They had an agreement to be no more than "friendly." And they were both abiding by it. There was no reason she couldn't enjoy his and Toby's company until the time came for her to be on her way.

Rick and Toby hung around the house that day. And so did Natalie, though she'd originally planned to drive to Travistown and visit her classroom, to clean out a few cabinets and get a head start on preparations for the fall. But she'd done some of that already, and she could handle the rest after her return.

And she certainly didn't need to shop for anything more to wear. Her closet was crammed with fabulous clothes. She was as ready as she'd ever be to look glamorous from Barcelona to Cairo and back again.

So she fished from the dock with Toby and Bernie, catching two minuscule trout, which Toby calmly removed from her hook and threw back in the water. Then there was lunch, a gourmet affair of peanut-butter-and-jelly sandwiches, juice boxes, apple slices and Creepy Crawlers fruit snacks. They made a picnic of it, spreading an old stadium blanket on the front lawn and sharing the fruit snacks with Bernie, who especially liked the purple spider ones. After the meal, they got out the ancient croquet set from the garage and set it up on the lawn. Then they batted the balls through the wickets with the old wooden mallets.

Later, Natalie's uncle Frank called. The housekeeper had left early, and Lindsay was at the hospital. He needed to make a quick trip into Minneapolis. Could he possibly leave Chelsea and Carter with her for a couple of hours?

"Sure, bring 'em on over."

Twenty minutes later, Frank dropped off his son and daughter. By then, it was nearing five o'clock. Rick and Natalie decided it would be fun to eat dinner outside. The menu would be hot dogs, potato chips and grape Kool-Aid. Rick was going to barbecue the dogs on the old stone barbecue that Grandpa Ben had built himself years ago.

"I love hot dogs," said Chelsea.

"Me too," agreed Carter.

Even Toby was smiling.

They all filed outside, each carrying something to contribute to the meal. Once everything had been brought out, Rick began stacking briquettes in the barbecue and Natalie set to work a few feet from him, taping a paper cloth to the redwood picnic table.

The kids stood around, not quite sure what to do with themselves yet. Carter was almost as reserved as Toby. But Chelsea made up for the silence of the boys.

"Don't you *talk?*" she demanded of Toby after a few minutes of nonstop chatter on her part.

Toby only stared at her, the way a traveler in a foreign land will often gape at the locals—as if he'd studied the language a little, but was totally unprepared for it to be spoken so *fast.*

"Well, don't you?"

Rick straightened from his work at the barbecue and started to speak. But Natalie moved swiftly, reaching his side in a few steps and putting a restraining hand on his arm.

"Did you hear me?" Chelsea demanded of Toby, speaking very slowly and deliberately now.

Solemnly Toby nodded.

"Well, then? Do you talk—or not?"

And Toby shook his head.

"Oh," said Chelsea, shrugging. "Okay." She took Toby's hand. "See that tree over there?" She pointed at a walnut tree near the garage.

Toby nodded.

"Let's go climb it." She turned to her brother. "Come on, Carter."

And the three of them sped off across the lawn, Bernie at their heels.

Natalie stared after them, grinning. Then she turned to look at him. "I thought it would be better if he answered for himself."

There was a half smile on his lips. "And, as usual, you were right."

She knew she should move away. But it felt so nice to touch him. And what she *should* do seemed pretty unimportant right then. She could hear the children laughing. And the teasing sigh of a breeze rippling the trees. And the cry of a bird somewhere.

But the sounds were muted, far away. Only Rick seemed near. Every line of his face was so vivid, so clear.

He drew in one deep, careful breath. She saw his chest expand beneath the polo shirt he was wearing, and then slowly contract when he let the breath out.

"Natalie."

"Yes?"

"I should get those briquettes going."

"Yes. Yes, I know." She let go of him and backed away.

The minute the contact was broken, she felt foolish. She shouldn't have done that; she'd held on way too long.

But he seemed totally unconcerned. As if nothing whatever had happened. He went right back to stacking his briquettes. And she told herself that if he didn't think she'd been out of line, then maybe she hadn't been. It was no big deal. She'd touched him to get his attention, so that he wouldn't steal Toby's right to answer Chelsea's questions for himself. And it had been nice, touching him. So she'd kept doing it, longer than she should have.

But it was no big deal. She wouldn't do it again.

When Rick served the hot dogs forty-five minutes later, the kids all ate as if they were starving. They had chocolate ice cream for dessert. Then they toted every thing back to the house, and the adults finished cleaning up while the kids gathered around the coffee table in the great room, putting puzzles together and playing with Toby's Emergency City.

Frank returned at seven to pick up Chelsea and Carter.

"Toby wants to come to our house sometime soon," Chelsea told Rick. "Will you bring him?"

Rick looked at Toby, who nodded enthusiastically.

"I'll give you a call next week," suggested Frank, "and we'll set something up."

"Sounds great," Rick said.

Natalie realized she'd miss that; next week, she'd be gone.

Which was great, really, wasn't it? The kids all got along, and Frank and Rick had seemed comfortable with each other right from the first. It was perfect. For everybody. And she'd be off doing the Mediterranean, so she'd be having a ball, too.

So why did it make her sad?

It didn't. It really didn't. She didn't feel sad at all.

Once Chelsea and Carter were gone, Natalie and Rick helped Toby finish the puzzle that he and the other kids had been working on. And then it was time for Toby to get ready for bed.

He had his bath and then Rick went to tuck him in. Natalie sat down on the sofa in the great room and picked up the remote, thinking that maybe she'd hang around down here for a while, if Rick didn't mind. She was switching between a rerun of "Home Improvement" and a murder mystery when Rick spoke from behind her.

"Natalie."

She turned, smiling, but the smile quickly faded when she saw his face. He stared at her, vacant-eyed and slack-jawed, as if he'd just had some terrible shock.

She was already on her feet. "My God, what's happened?"

"He asked for you."

"Who, Toby?"

Rick nodded.

She frowned, trying to understand. "Well, fine, I'll be glad to say good-night to him."

"Natalie." His voice was low and rough. "I said Toby *asked* for you."

It took a moment for that to sink in. "In *words?*"

Rick nodded again. "Out of nowhere, in a whisper, he said, 'Could Natalie come kiss me?'"

Behind her, on the television, a string of commercials had begun. Natalie grabbed the remote from the coffee table and switched the thing off.

Then she turned back to Rick.

The look of shock had been replaced by a broad smile. "Will you? Go kiss him?"

She tossed the remote on a side table. "You bet I will."

In Toby's bedroom, Bernie was already stretched out on the floor. Toby lay in the bed, under the airplane quilt.

Natalie went and sat on the edge. "Your dad says you asked for me."

Toby nodded.

"He said you wanted a kiss."

Another nod.

Natalie bent and brushed her lips against his forehead. Before she could pull away, two small arms closed around her neck. Toby gave her a squeeze and pressed his soft cheek to hers.

"I had a good time today," she whispered.

In answer, he gave her another squeeze.

Then she pulled back and tucked the covers closer around him. "You sleep tight, now." She switched off the airplane lamp.

Toby turned on his side and closed his eyes.

Rick was waiting on the threshold. When she moved past him, he quietly reached in and pulled the door closed.

Then he leaned back against the door and grinned at her. "There should be a celebration. Will you celebrate with me?" His eyes were shining, and his face was flushed.

She simply couldn't refuse him—not that she wanted to. "Sure."

They headed for the great room. "Dr. Dawkins—that's Toby's psychiatrist—said this would happen," Rick told her in a hushed, excited tone before they were halfway down the hall. "At Toby's last visit, she *said* he'd start talking. And she told me that when he did, I should be careful to let him find his own pace with it, not to push him, you know?"

"Yes, that makes sense."

They were standing near the sofa by then. He was grinning at her. And then he blinked. "Champagne. We should have champagne."

She smiled and nodded.

He spun on his heel and started for the kitchen—but then he stopped and threw up his hands. "I don't have any champagne. Can you believe it? People *always* have champagne at times like this."

His enthusiasm was contagious. "How about brandy?" she suggested. "There's a bottle of Courvoisier in the pantry."

He frowned. "I don't know..." She could see that the idea of drinking brandy didn't thrill him. She was glad. Joel had been a brandy drinker—though he'd always insisted that she call it cognac. As a Christmas gift two years before, he'd bought her a set of balloon glasses, so that she could serve it *properly.*

She put Joel from her mind. "How about white wine? There's something German in the back of the refrigerator."

He laughed. "Something *German?*"

"Yep. Aunt Lindsay brought it over a while back. It's a Riesling of some kind."

He shrugged. "Sure, let's go for the Riesling."

He found the wine and opened it, while she brought down the glasses. They put some cheddar and wheat crackers on a cutting board, moved Toby's puzzle and his Emergency City onto a pair of TV trays and set the goodies on the coffee table.

Once they'd settled on the sofa, Rick filled their glasses and raised his high. "To my favorite landlady," he said, and drank. Then he looked in his glass. "Hey. This isn't half-bad."

She sipped from her own glass. It *was* good. "Aunt Lindsay has excellent taste."

Rick raised his glass again. "To Aunt Lindsay, then."

"I'll drink to that." And she did.

"What next?"

"Huh?"

"Who should we drink to next? I want to drink to everybody. I feel that good."

"We only have one bottle of wine."

"Then it will go fast. I have it. Your mother. We should drink to your mother. I really like her."

That surprised Natalie. People said her mother was beautiful, or difficult, or intimidating. But they rarely simply liked her. "You do?"

He nodded. "She's kind. You saw how she was with Toby."

"She does love children."

"But she's fragile, too." He rested an arm along the back of the sofa. "I think that worries you."

Natalie took another big sip. "Mostly, people don't notice that my mother is fragile. She's so beautiful, that's all they see."

"You're evading."

"I am? How?"

"I said I think you worry about your mother. Is that true?"

"All right," she conceded. "Yes, I worry about her. Sometimes I think she's not equipped to deal with life on her own. She was very young when my father swept her off her feet. And he's dominated every aspect of her life since then. Until recently, that *is*."

"But she is managing."

"Yes. She's managing. Is this some kind of lecture you're giving me here? That you think I should stop worrying about my mother, or something?"

He raised a hand, palm up, and endeavored to look

solemn. "No lecture. I promise. An observation, that's all."

"Well." She grinned at him. The air seemed to be humming with their mutual excitement over Toby's breakthrough. It was a wonderful, shining moment. "An observation is perfectly acceptable."

"Good." He raised his glass again. "To Erica Fortune, then."

"To my mother." And they both drank.

He refilled their glasses. "Now, it's your turn."

"My turn?"

"Make a toast."

"Oh, Rick."

"Come on."

She lifted her glass. "To Toby, then."

"I will definitely drink to that." And he did. After he swallowed, he instructed, "Now, make another one."

And for some reason, she thought of her grandma Kate. And of how she missed her. And how it hurt, knowing such strength and wisdom were no longer in the world. She felt for the rosebud charm that hung around her neck, hidden by the collar of her shirt.

Rick reached across the distance between them and lifted her chin. "Hey. This is supposed to be a celebration."

She tried to look away, but she didn't try very hard. "It's the wine."

He smiled, still holding her chin. "It's too soon to be feeling the effects of the wine."

His touch was warm, and his eyes were so kind. She couldn't resist him, didn't want to resist him.

"I miss my grandma." Was that her own voice? It sounded so small.

Rick's hand slid upward. He brushed her cheek. She

didn't know that a tear had escaped her lids until she felt him rub the moisture away.

"I'm being silly," she said, but she leaned a little closer to him.

The brushing touch became a caress. "No, I think you just...miss your grandma."

"Oh, Rick."

His hand slid around to cup the back of her neck. She couldn't have said whether he pulled her toward him—or she moved of her own accord. It was probably a combination of the two.

But suddenly, their lips were so close. His breath was warm and sweet on her face. And then, before she could stop and think about it, she herself eliminated that extra fraction of an inch.

Her mouth touched his.

"Rick." She said his name against his parted lips. "I didn't..."

"Shh... I think you did."

And then his mouth was on hers, moving so gently, cherishingly. His hand massaged the back of her neck. It felt so good, so absolutely right.

Natalie heard a little moaning sound, and then realized it had come from her own throat. Her mouth opened a little. His tongue slipped in, just to the inner surface of her lips. He tasted her there, with a secret, knowing, moist caress.

Heat bloomed in her belly. It was wonderful. She wanted it never to stop.

But then, with a low, regretful sigh, he pulled back. His hand fell away, and he looked at her. It was a long, slow, measuring look.

"Make your toast."

Natalie knew they'd gone too far. To salvage the situation now, she should set her wine down, stand from the sofa and say good-night.

But, oh, sweet Lord, how he could kiss. She couldn't remember ever being kissed like that.

With such frank desire—and yet such restraint.

It was terribly seductive. And she wanted more. She wanted to go with it, sink into it and let it carry her where it might.

Yet she couldn't. She had to consider what would happen later. She'd sworn to herself that she wasn't going to get herself into another losing situation with a man. And this had all the earmarks of being just that. They had two more days together in this house. And then she was leaving. What would those two days be like if they did something...irrevocable tonight?

They'd been managing so well, too, with their little agreement to be *friendly*....

"Make your toast, Natalie." His eyes had changed again. They didn't look kind anymore. Fire was burning in them, and she knew it was a fire that could consume her. Deliciously. "Make your toast, or get up and go."

She stared at him, wide-eyed, amazed that he was putting into words the very choice she'd just been secretly pondering.

"Everything's been working out well, hasn't it?" He spoke more of her own thoughts aloud, in a low, intense voice. "Everything's been just the way you wanted it. Since we talked the other night, we've been getting along fine. I've respected your wishes. I've kept myself on the safe side of that invisible line you've drawn. But I really don't want to stay on the safe side. I never made any secret of that."

She gulped.

"Did I?"

She shook her head.

"You invited that kiss, just now."

"Um, I..."

"Just admit it. You wanted to kiss me. And you did."

Slowly she nodded.

"You crossed the line yourself. And I was the one who stopped it. Now I'm back where you put me, on the other side of the line from you. But if you give me any more encouragement, I'm not going to stay where you put me. I'm going to make love with you." His voice had turned silky. It rubbed along her nerve endings, setting off sparks. "Do you understand?"

She did. Perfectly. "Yes."

"But it's your choice. So make it."

"I..."

"Make your choice."

It was all so bewildering. On the one hand, she felt so comfortable with Rick, much more comfortable than she'd ever felt with Joel, or with any other man, for that matter. She and Rick seemed to approach life the same way. They agreed on so many things. And for the past couple of days, while they'd been getting along, when something needed doing, they'd both just pitched in until the task was accomplished. Life went smoothly when she was around him.

Yet, on the other hand, Rick *excited* her. In frightening and overwhelming ways. Therein lay the danger. It would be so easy for him to mean too much to her.

Joel Baines had hurt her deeply. But she feared that Rick Dalton could break her heart.

He was through waiting for her to make up her mind. She could see it in his eyes.

"Fine." He set his glass on the coffee table and moved to rise. "*I'll* go, then."

She put her hand on his arm, felt the heat and the tension. "No. Stay." He went absolutely still. She whispered, "Please."

He sank back to the couch. "If I stay..."

"I know." She swallowed, and could hardly believe her own boldness when she said, "We'll make love."

"Is that what you want?"

"Yes." The word came out not much more than a whisper. But he heard it. She knew that he did. She raised her glass. "To Grandma Kate."

He found his own glass, then met her gaze as he lifted it high. "To Kate."

They both drank.

Eleven

When she lowered her glass, Rick took it from her. He set it on the coffee table and set his own beside it.

He knew she was uncertain about this. He could see it in her eyes. He should probably back off now, walk away, spare them both the possible consequences that making love could bring.

But he wanted Natalie, had wanted her from the first, with a power and certainty that shocked the hell out of him. In a few days, she'd be leaving. Tonight might represent his only chance with her.

And he'd be damned if he'd walk away from it.

There was one more hurdle to get over: the problem any responsible man had to face, even though the price might be everything he'd just fought to gain.

"I'm not prepared. I don't have any—"

She flushed bright red and cut in before he could finish. "It's okay. I do. Upstairs. Joel and I, we used them. Sometimes. And I have some left." She closed her eyes. "Oh, God."

He reached out, took her hand. "Don't. It's okay."

"I feel so—"

"It's really okay, Natalie."

She opened her eyes, looked down at their joined hands and then up at him. "It is?"

He nodded. And then, very slowly, so as not to startle her, he touched her face with his free hand, traced her nose and her cheekbones, her brows and her lips. Her breath, against his fingers, was warm and a little ragged. Her lips moved under his touch. He leaned closer, breathing in the scent of her.

And then he put his mouth where his fingers had been, over hers.

Their second kiss was long and lazy. He explored her mouth, every inch of it, inside and out. She seemed to melt into him as he kissed her. And he gathered her close, feeling the softness of her breasts against his chest, tasting her more deeply.

Eventually, to keep from moving too fast, he broke the kiss. He took her shoulders, held her away and made her look at him.

Her sweet face was flushed, and her eyes were soft with a tender, bewildered desire. The sight increased his arousal, making him groan and pull her close again, hungrily reclaiming her mouth, loving the feel of her, so warm and firm and pliant to his touch.

Her white shirt buttoned down the front. He went to work on those buttons, remembering all the nights since he'd come to her house when he'd lain alone in bed and gone crazy imagining doing just what he was doing now.

Soon enough, he was smoothing the shirt open, revealing the necklace with the rosebud charm, as well as her lacy pink bra. He couldn't resist. He lowered his head and kissed her, finding her nipple right through the bra.

She moaned and arched toward him. He clutched her closer, then made himself loosen his grip a little, as he mentally counted to ten.

"Rick..." She was looking at him, her face flushed, her eyes bright with need.

The pink lace drew him like a magnet. He touched the small clasp between her breasts. She gasped. With a little maneuvering, he had it undone. Her soft lips were parted, and her breath came sweet and fast as he pushed the scrap of lace out of his way. He cupped her naked breast, which swelled invitingly, looking impossibly soft and round in his hand. And then he lowered his head and took it in his mouth.

She cried aloud and surged up toward him. He laid her back along the couch, following her down, suckling her as she moaned and rubbed herself against him, and he realized he might go insane if he didn't have her naked beneath him soon.

His hand strayed down between them, seeking the soft, secret place between her thighs. Even through her cotton shorts, he felt the heat and wetness. He rubbed her, tauntingly, and she lifted herself to his hand. He felt for her zipper.

And she grabbed his wrist.

He pulled back, breathing hard, a hot stab of frustration piercing the haze of desire. If she'd changed her mind now...

She was biting her lip. "What if Toby...?"

And he knew she was right. They were crazy to go further here in the great room, with its bank of dark windows looking out on the night and his son just down the hall. They should find a more private place.

"Your room?"

She nodded. "But we should check on Toby first."

He agreed with that. He made himself sit back. Then he watched, aching, wanting to order her not to cover herself, as she straightened the clothes he'd undone.

They tiptoed to Toby's room and peeked in. He was fast asleep, facing toward the door. The sound of his breathing came to them, even and slow.

On the floor, Bernie looked up, ears lifted, his big, wise

eyes going from Rick to Natalie. And then, undoubtedly having decided that they needed nothing from him, he laid his head back on his paws and shut his eyes.

Carefully Rick pulled the door closed. Natalie was right there at his side. The scent of her taunted him— flowers and musk.

He pulled her to him. She came without resistance, giving him the soft length of herself, releasing one sweet, eager sigh. He put his hand at the small of her back and pressed her firmly into him, rubbing himself against her, imprinting his body on hers.

She gave a little groan. He sipped the sound from her lips, shoving his fingers into the dark, fragrant silk of her hair and cupping her face, so that he could kiss her more deeply.

For a suspended moment, she pressed herself close, and then she was grasping his wrists again, pulling back. He made a noise that could only be called a growl, and tried to pull her close again.

She resisted. "Upstairs. Please, Rick…"

And he let her lead him by the hand, to the stairs and up to her bedroom. She pushed the door open and pulled him inside.

It was a big room, with a bay window that fronted the side lawn and another that looked out over the dark expanse of the lake. Through the haze of his hunger for her, he was aware of dark, expensive, old-fashioned furniture, of good silk rugs and a lace-canopied four-poster covered in a pale yellow, silky spread. She switched on a small lamp atop one of the cherrywood dressers.

And then she fumbled in a drawer of that dresser. He knew what she was after. When she found the small packets, she closed the dresser drawer and turned to him, her eyes full of questions, enchantingly unsure.

He approached her and took the packets from her. Then he wrapped his arms around her and pulled her close.

She came stiffly against him at first, and then the melting began, as he covered her lips with his. Kissing her every step of the way, he took her to the bed. He set the condoms on the night stand. And then, with eager hands, he unbuttoned buttons, unhooked hooks, coaxing and cajoling until he'd taken all of her clothes away.

Naked, she tried to cover herself. He took her hands, turned them over and kissed the soft inner swells at the base of her thumbs.

"Oh, Rick..."

"Just don't hide. There's no reason to hide. Not from me. Not ever."

"No man has ever made me feel like you do."

"Good." He squeezed both of her hands, then stepped back. For a moment, he allowed himself to look his fill at soft, high breasts, a long sweep of waist, and the dark, shiny curls between slim legs. Then, swiftly, he began removing his own clothes.

She watched him while he did it, her eyes wide and wondering. Once he was done, he reached for her again.

And when the whole nude length of her touched him, he knew their first time was going to lack the finesse and tenderness he'd hoped to bring to it.

He muttered her name, control slipping away, and then he kissed her, hard and deep. She returned the kiss eagerly, her sweet tongue mating with his.

They fell across the bed. He touched her. She gave a mewling, needful cry and her body bowed up toward his hand.

She was so wet, so silky and hot. And he couldn't wait. He reached out, groping, until he found one of the condoms. By some miracle, he managed to roll it on over his straining hardness.

And then he was settling between her soft thighs. He glanced down, into beautiful, wide, bewildered eyes. And he thrust in.

She moaned. And she wrapped those long girl-next-door legs around him, lifting up to him like the swelling of the sweetest, most enveloping wave. And the rest was only the scent of her, the feel of her, the very center of her that, he knew as he surged in and out of her, he must somehow reach.

After an eternity that passed in an instant, her body began rising toward climax. He felt her silky inner muscles, closing and opening around him, milking him. He heard her startled, ecstatic cry. And he was gone, lost, finished, falling into the trough of the wave, then rising to the crest on a final, triumphant shout.

He emptied himself into her, emptied everything, pressing deep, pulsing hard, until there was nothing left but her softness all around him, cradling him, holding him close.

For an immeasurable time after that, he lay limp and boneless on her soft, giving body. Then he asked in a whisper if he was too heavy.

She sighed and shook her head.

He levered upward and stroked the damp hair away from her brow. And then he couldn't help kissing her, a kiss that was so immeasurably sweet, because her mouth gave to him, opening, letting him in.

He slid to the side, pulling out of her, enjoying the way she clung to him, as if she didn't want to let him go. And then he put his hand on her, partly in reassurance, and also because he wanted to make her rise to him again.

And she did, swiftly, lifting her hips, crying out in that bewildered way that he'd already grown to love. As if she didn't understand what was happening to her, as if, in spite of the fears that made her want to hold back from him, she couldn't hold back—she was totally and completely his.

Just as she hit the crest for the second time, he lowered his head and put his mouth where his hand had been, at the secret, pulsing heart of her. She shoved her fingers in his hair, holding him there and pushing herself up to him, frantic, helpless, shuddering endlessly. He wanted to kiss her like that forever, so deeply and intimately, to be lost for eternity in the sweet liquid center of her.

She let go of his head with one final, quivering sigh. He lingered, still kissing her, until she pushed at him a little, sated, oversensitized now.

With a final brushing caress of his lips on the pale skin of her belly, he left her just long enough to dispose of the used condom. Then he stretched out beside her, gathering her close, turning her so that she fit back against him, spoon-fashion.

Her hair tickled his nose. He smoothed it, and pulled her closer. Then he closed his eyes. He felt the long sigh leave her body and knew she had closed her eyes, too. They drifted for a while, somewhere between dream and waking.

But eventually, he started caressing her again, and then he reached for another condom. He slid into her smoothly, as if coming home. They rocked together, long, slow and deep. And this time, when the end came, he had no idea whether it started with him or in her.

After a time, when their breathing had slowed, he left her once more, returning within minutes, finding her under the covers that time. He slid in beside her and pulled her against him.

Held close in Rick's arms, Natalie stirred.

Rick drew her closer. "Hmm?" he asked in a heavy, sleepy voice. "Okay?"

"Yes. I just…I have to go to the bathroom."

His arms loosened their hold on her. She slid from the bed, sensing that he watched her as she walked away, but not daring to look back and see whether she was right.

In the blue-tiled bathroom, she switched on the light and relieved herself. Then, at the sink, as she washed her hands, Natalie couldn't help looking at herself in the mirror. Her hair was all tangled around her face, which looked flushed and droopy-eyed. Her mascara had smudged under her eyes.

She thought of the things she'd just done with Rick, in the other room. And her whole body hummed with remembered pleasure. She could hardly believe how it had been. Never in her life had she moaned and cried out like that—or had it go on and on, had it not really be over when she thought it was over. Never had a man so eagerly kissed her in such private places—and then wanted to keep on kissing her, even after it was clear that she'd achieved satisfaction.

Really, now that she stood here in the harsh light of her own bathroom and played it over in her mind, it was all…just a little too good to be true.

With a tiny groan that was part confusion and part embarrassment, Natalie pressed both hands to her cheeks, remembering that first day when Rick and Toby had come to stay at her house—that first day out on the boat, when Rick had almost kissed her, and she'd pulled away just in time. Had she known even then that one kiss was all it would take?

It certainly seemed that way, because after that first kiss on the sofa in the great room, her logical mental processes had fled, leaving her pretty much brainless. All that had been left in her head was one thought: She wanted Rick, wanted to know what it would be like to lie in his arms.

Now she knew. It was wonderful. Incredible. Better than anything she'd known before, in her admittedly limited experience of intimacy with men.

But really, how well did she know Rick? Certainly not well enough to go to bed with him.

She remembered what Joel had said to her, when he told her it was over between them. *You're a nice woman, Natalie, and there's no one more dependable. But I have to be frank. You're not very exciting. And I think I deserve some excitement in my life....*

A little while ago, Rick had seemed pretty excited by her. But could she believe him?

She and Joel hadn't made love until they'd been dating for months and months. Rick had been in her house for mere weeks, and most of that time he'd spent treating her as if he hated her. For the past three days—count 'em, *three*—he'd been nice to her. And now he was lying in her bed, in the other room.

Natalie's cheeks felt as if they were on fire. She turned on the cold tap all the way and splashed the cool water on her face, rubbing her fingers under eyes to get rid of the smudges left by her mascara. Then, after scrubbing her face dry with a towel, she grabbed a brush from the counter and dragged it through her tangled hair.

She was acting like a fool, she knew it. What was done was done.

And it had been beautiful. It *had*. There was no reason she had to spoil it for herself with all these negative second thoughts. The thing for her to do right now was to pull herself together and go back to the other room.

But she couldn't quite do it. She paced back and forth across the blue tiles, approaching the door to the bedroom and then turning away from it, unable to reach out and twist the knob.

Finally, with a long sigh, she sank to the edge of the tub and put her head in her hands.

The knock on the door came just a few seconds later. "Natalie?"

She longed to call out, "Go away!" but knew how utterly foolish that would sound.

Slowly, the door swung inward. Rick was on the other side of it, naked as she was, a worried frown making a crease between his dark brows. His body was so fine, wide-shouldered, deep-chested, with long, strong legs and...

Embarrassment flooded through her. She made herself look away, wondering what in the world she was doing here, in her own bathroom, with this incredibly handsome naked man. It wasn't like her at all.

As each moment passed, what had happened in the other room seemed more and more like a dream. Something not really real. Something from which she was now waking, to face the consequences of an act that she never should have allowed to happen.

"Rick, I..."

Uneasiness tightened like a fist around Rick's heart. He didn't like the look on her face. "What?"

He watched as she glanced down at herself, wrapping her arms across her breasts, hunching her shoulders—

trying to cover herself. Not too long ago, he'd asked her not to do that. And she'd said that she wouldn't.

"Could you...give me my robe? It's on the back of the door."

He pulled on the door, so that he could check the back of it. Sure enough, the robe hung there. He lifted it from its hook and tossed it to her.

She stood, catching it as it flew through the air. "Thank you." Swiftly she stuck her hands in the sleeves.

Judging by the look on her face, something grim was going to happen. Rick decided he'd just as soon not face it naked. So he turned from her and went back to the other room, where he picked up his jeans from the floor and yanked them on. He was buttoning them up when she appeared in the bathroom doorway.

"Rick, I..." Again, as before, she couldn't seem to think of what to say next.

Not long ago, he'd been certain that everything was going to work out fine. His certainty was fast slipping away. "What is it? Just say it."

"Rick, I... We..." She looked at him hopelessly, and then she dragged in a breath and let out words he'd been secretly fearing she might say. "It was a mistake, what we just did."

He fisted his hands at his sides, determined to stay reasonable. "I thought it was a choice. A choice you made voluntarily."

"It was. Yes. But, you see, as much as I sometimes tell myself that I'm going to be bold and try a one-night stand sometime, I never really expected I'd ever do it. It's just...not the way I am."

He took in a deep breath and let it out very slowly. "Is that what this was to you? A one-night stand?"

She stuck her hands in the pockets of her robe, then

looked at him with her head tipped to the side. "Was it a one-night stand to you?"

He wanted to shout at her that she could damn well answer his question before she hit him with one of her own. But he didn't. He didn't trust himself to speak. So he granted her a tight shake of his head.

"Oh. I see." She didn't sound relieved.

He clenched his fists harder, knowing that the real zinger had to be coming up next.

She hit him with it. "But you had to know that a one-night stand is all it could be."

"Why?" It came out a hoarse croak.

She bit her pretty lower lip. "Well, as I've already explained to you, I'm not equipped right now to get involved with anyone. Especially not someone like you."

The last thing he really wanted to know was what the hell she meant by *that*, but still he heard himself asking quietly, "Someone like me?"

"Yes." Her throat moved convulsively as she swallowed. "Someone so…good-looking and sexy. Someone who will use me."

He felt as if she'd kneed him in the groin. "Use you."

She nodded. "Let's be honest, okay? I know there must be something, some deeper reason why you made love to me. I mean, come on." She spread her arms to the sides. Now that she had the robe wrapped around her, she seemed to feel safe doing that. "Look at me."

He did, long and piercingly, keeping his expression blank.

She couldn't take his scrutiny. Her eyes slid away to focus blindly on one of her cherrywood dressers. "You know and I know I'm not the kind of woman that men lose their heads over."

Now what could he say to that? If he argued that he

damn well *had* lost his head over her, she'd call him a liar. "Natalie..."

Still looking at the dresser, she threw up a hand. "No. Stop. Let's get real. You could have a lot of women." She bit her lip, and made herself face him. "Is it Toby? Is it that you need a certain kind of woman, someone who'd be a good mother to him?"

It was too much. She seemed determined to put herself down—and make him into a bad guy. Rick's anger was growing. He tried to will it away, to remain reasonable and logical. Carefully he sat on the edge of the rumpled bed. "Is that really what you think, that I'm looking for a woman to take care of Toby?"

"I don't know. I'm trying to understand."

He couldn't help doubting that. "Are you?"

"Yes. Of course." She frowned, thinking. "Is it who I am? That I'm a Fortune? Or is it money? Do you need money? Just...just tell me now. I want the truth."

Now she *was* calling him a liar. The anger he was trying not to feel burned hotter. Very casually, he leaned back on an elbow among the tangled blankets. "All right. Let's see." He laid on the sarcasm. "I don't need money. And I don't give a damn what your last name is. I do, however, love the way you are with Toby. So maybe that's it." He sat up straight. "I'm just looking for a live-in baby-sitter. And you'd be perfect. So I had sex with you, to seduce you to my will."

Her face paled. She was only a few feet from him, standing by her little vanity table. Slowly she sank into the chair there. "You can try making a joke of it. But I have to know. Is that really it?"

He stared into her eyes, reminding himself bleakly that she was insecure, that she'd been hurt badly in the not-too-distant past, that he should go easy, be gentle, do whatever he could to reassure her.

But, damn it, what had happened in this room tonight had made a vast difference to him. Too much difference, really. He felt exposed. Vulnerable. And he was in no condition to fall all over himself trying to convince her that he wasn't the gold-digging loser she seemed to think any man who went after her would have to be.

"Rick. Answer me."

If this went any further, he would say something he'd regret. He felt it in his bones.

He tried to remember how it had been earlier, how beautiful and right.

But somehow, that made it all the worse, that she could turn on him now.

He stood. "Look, Natalie. Maybe you're right. Maybe we've made a mistake."

She pulled her robe tighter around her, hunched her shoulders and bent her head, so that she looked small and lost in the white, fluffy folds. "Yes. Yes, I think we have."

The urge to grab her and shake her rocketed through him. He folded his arms across his chest and gritted his teeth, biting back the harsh words that wanted so badly to be said.

She looked up again, her eyes wide and wounded. "I think I should leave. I'll stay at my father's for the next couple of days. It would be too difficult, I think, for me to stay here."

He thought of Vanessa then. How totally hopeless it had been to argue with her. Vanessa would get an idea in her head, and there would be no reasoning with her. After those first months of infatuation, their life together had been pure hell, so much so that he'd thought he'd learned his lesson.

But then he'd met Natalie. He'd been certain she was as different from Vanessa as day was from darkness.

Dalton, he thought bleakly, welcome to the middle of the night.

"Rick? Did you hear me?"

He nodded.

"I'm going to go on over to my father's house."

"Suit yourself," he said curtly. Then he gathered up the rest of his clothes and got the hell out.

Twelve

The minute the door closed behind Rick, Natalie stood. But her legs felt weak. So she sank back onto the little vanity chair.

She had told Rick she would leave. And she would. In just a minute, as soon as she got a grip on herself.

Her body hummed with nervous energy. She closed her eyes, breathed deep and slow, trying to calm herself.

But then, on the dark inside of her eyelids, she saw Rick, while they were making love, looking at her as if she were the most beautiful, most desirable woman in the world....

With a little groan of misery, she jumped to her feet. She marched to her closet and got down a small leather suitcase, which she carried back to the bed. Swiftly she plowed through her dresser drawers, finding underwear and socks and casual clothes enough to last for a couple of days.

Of course, she'd have to return to pack up her fancy wardrobe of vacation outfits before she left for the airport. But she could wait until Sunday, late in the day, to take care of that. And then she could come right up here, to her own rooms, where she'd stay until she finished packing her trunks. There was no reason she'd have to deal with Rick at all.

She thought of Toby, of the fact that he'd actually spoken tonight. He'd asked for *her*. His little arms had felt so good when he wrapped them close around her neck. Oh, she was going to miss him. She was going to miss him terribly.

With a tiny cry, she sank onto the edge of the bed and put her face in her hands. After a moment of fierce concentration, she felt calmer again.

She lifted her head, straightened her shoulders. She would have her emotions completely under control by Sunday. And she'd say goodbye to Toby then.

Nothing was changed by what had happened between herself and Rick tonight—nothing that mattered, anyway. She would go on her cruise and Rick and Toby would take care of her house and her dog, just as it had been planned from the first. The only thing different would be the two days she spent at the estate.

Natalie stood once more and looked down at her suitcase. Mentally she ticked off what she saw and decided she had everything she would need for now. She zipped the thing shut. Then she went to the bathroom, where she stepped out of her robe and into the shower.

As the water streamed down over her, she told herself that she would forget all about tonight in no time. It had just been one of those things. She'd been so confused lately; nothing seemed to be the way it should be anymore. It had probably been bound to happen, that she'd do something foolish and risky—such as falling for her handsome tenant—and then have to suffer the consequences.

Not that there would be any consequences. Not really serious ones, anyway. Neither she nor Rick was otherwise committed. And they'd been careful to practice safe sex.

As soon as she'd had her shower and thrown on some jeans and a clean shirt, Natalie was ready to go. She decided to take her car. Technically, Rick was entitled to the use of the ski boat. And she might need her car in the next couple of days, anyway.

At the gate to the estate, she had to wait what seemed like forever for that new housekeeper to buzz her in. When she reached the sweeping front drive, all the floodlights were on, bathing the imposing facade in a wash of artificial brightness. After she stopped the car, she waited for a moment, thinking that this time she wouldn't disappoint Edgar; he could open her door for her.

But Edgar didn't come. Silly of her. He was probably sound asleep. She noticed the shiny black sports car waiting near the front walk. It looked like one of the cars her father liked to use when he decided to do his own driving.

The new housekeeper answered her knock. Her gray hair was in a braid down her back, and she clutched the facings of a dark-colored robe.

"I'm sorry to wake you."

"It's no problem, miss."

"Is my father here?"

"I really couldn't say. He went out earlier, but he could have returned by now. I've been in my room for the past hour or so. Until you, no one has rung for me."

Natalie shifted her bag from her left hand to her right, trying to decide what to do next. She felt more than a little numb, actually. She was just trying to keep moving, so that she wouldn't have to think too much.

"May I take your suitcase?"

She clutched the bag a little tighter. "Um, no. I think I'll just go on up to one of the guest rooms. I can carry my own things."

"The blue room is freshly aired."

"Yes. Fine. I'll take the blue room."

"May I help you to settle in?"

"No, really. That's not necessary. I've disturbed you enough."

"It's no bother."

"Thank you. Really. No."

"As you wish. Good night, then." She was already walking away.

"Good night," Natalie murmured to the woman's retreating back. The housekeeper quickly disappeared down a side hall, headed for the kitchen and the servants' wing behind it.

Once the woman was gone, Natalie started for the central staircase. But then she hesitated. She was all keyed up, and unlikely to be able to sleep. She knew that she would lie there in the strange bed, staring at the ceiling and trying not to remember the feel of Rick's hands on her skin, trying not to think of all the ways he had touched her, of how he really had seemed to *like* touching her—almost as much as she'd liked being touched by him. Trying not to wonder whether she might just have walked out on the best thing that had ever happened to her…

No, sleep was not going to come easily. She set her suitcase and her shoulder bag on the shining expanse of floor and headed for the library, in search of a book to help her to make it through the long night ahead.

She thought it odd when she reached the tall carved double doors and saw the sliver of light peeking out from under them. The staff was usually careful about leaving lights on when no one was using them. But then she shrugged. The woman who'd just let her in was proof that at least some of the staff were new. And her father, with all his current worries, probably wasn't nearly as exacting as Grandma Kate used to be.

Natalie pulled back one of the two doors and stepped over the threshold.

Her father was there, slouched in his chair at the big desk on the other side of the room. At the sound of the door opening, he raised his head.

Natalie stared. It was hard to absorb what she saw. He looked very bad. His skin was gray, and his eyes were red-rimmed, with dark pouches beneath them. His hair stood up in spikes, as if he'd been dragging his fingers through it. There was a bright bruise on his chin. Long red scratches marked his neck. He had tossed the jacket of his suit over the back of his chair, and his white silk shirt was rumpled and torn at the shoulder—and spotted with what looked very much like dried blood. In front of him on the desk, a half-empty bottle of Chivas waited, beside a short, thick crystal glass.

He squinted at her, leaning closer over the desk. "Nat?"

It took her a moment to find her voice. Her grandpa Ben aside, her father was the strongest, steadiest man she'd ever known. To see him reduced to this caused an awful, hollow feeling down in the deepest core of her.

He muttered her name for the second time.

"Yes, Dad." She spoke carefully, gently. "It's me."

"Well. Welcome." He picked up the bottle of Scotch and sloshed some into the glass. "C'mon in." He grabbed the glass and knocked half the drink back, gasping after he swallowed.

Natalie regarded him warily, trying to decide what exactly she should do.

He grunted. "Don't give me that look. I got it unner control. You know your dad. Always unner control." He studied the glass, as if there were something terribly interesting about it. And then he squinted at Natalie again.

"Well. What's the matter? Isn't it late? Why're you here?"

"I just…I'm here for the night. Well, until Monday morning, actually. Is that okay?"

He blinked owlishly at her and forked a hand through the gray spikes of his hair. "'Course it's okay. You've always got a place here." He frowned. "But you still didn't say what you're doing here."

There was pressure in her chest. Pain for him. What could have happened, for him to be sitting here, in a torn, bloody shirt, drinking himself senseless in the middle of the night? She shouldn't want to know. She'd told herself she was staying away from the endless problems in the family.

But this looked like something much worse than just a *problem*. This looked scary. This looked very, very bad.

"You gonna stand there in the doorway staring at me with those big sad eyes all night long?"

"No, Dad. Of course not." She turned and closed the door behind her.

He gestured at a chair. "Have a seat. An' have a drink." He was already pouring himself another. "You want Scotch?"

"No."

"Well." He gestured again. "Cabinet's over there. Help yourself. Whatever you want."

"No, thanks."

He lifted a shoulder, the one that wasn't spotted with blood. "Suit yourself."

Cautiously she approached the desk. "Dad, I think you've had enough."

He snorted as he drank again.

She moved around the desk, until she was standing beside his big swivel chair. He was just setting his glass down when she took the arm of the chair and spun it so that he faced her. His eyes rolled a little, as if the sudden movement had dizzied him, and then he leveled a pitiful imitation of his old, hard stare on her.

"Nat. Watch yourself."

She saw then that he'd been cut somehow, beneath the torn shirt. "Dad. You're hurt...." Instinctively wanting to comfort, she reached out.

He flinched back, turned his bobbling head to look at his torn shirt and injured shoulder. Then he grunted and waved a hand. "'S nothing. A scratch." He tried to reach for his drink.

She held on to the arms of the chair, and knelt before him. "Dad. What's going on here? What's happened?"

He peered down at her, scowling. And then his face went lax. He sucked in a deep breath. "'S not your problem. You don't want to know." He jerked in the chair, as if trying to break free of her grip. But he didn't put much energy into it.

And she held on tight. "Yes, Dad. I do. I do want to know."

He reached out, weakly, and his hand brushed her cheek. "Innocent Nat. With her big heart, looking at the world through her rose-colored glasses."

"Talk to me. Please."

"You still love those Disney movies?"

"Dad..."

"I heard you got rid of that creep you were seeing. Joel."

"Yes, I got rid of Joel."

"Good. You can do better."

"Dad. Tell me what's happened to you."

He looked away.

"Dad. Please."

He was shaking his head. "You don't want to be...involved."

"Yes, I do." Her voice stunned her with its absolute conviction. "I do want to be involved." And in spite of what she'd been telling herself for months now, she realized it was true. "I *need* to be involved." And that was true, too.

Jake scrubbed a hand down his face. "No. Not good. Shouldn't. God. Shouldn't..."

But she knew that he wanted to tell it, whatever it was. That he wanted to get it out. "Tell me, Dad. It's all right. You have to tell someone. And I'm family. I love you, and you can trust me. Tell me."

"God. Nat..."

"Come on. I'm listening."

He muttered a name.

"What, Dad? Who?"

"Monica," he said low. "That bitch Monica Malone."

Natalie swallowed and wondered whether she should stop pushing him to confide in her. She felt like a little girl again. She wanted her father to be strong and her family to be whole and perfect. She wanted her innocence back. She wanted everything the way it used to be.

But it wasn't the way it used to be. And it was probably about time she came to grips with that.

"What about her, Dad?" she coaxed. "What about Monica Malone?"

"Blackmailing bitch," he muttered, then covered his face with his hands.

Natalie reached up, took his wrists and peeled them away from his tired, gray face. Everyone in the family assumed the woman must have something on her father, but Jake had never admitted it. Until now. "Monica Malone's been blackmailing you?"

Jake groaned. "All that damn stock. She demanded the stock."

"Your personal stocks that you turned over to her? Is that what you mean?"

He nodded, pressed his fist to his mouth.

"You say it was blackmail? Blackmail for what?"

He blinked, peered hard at her, then looked away. "Need 'nother drink."

"No, Dad. You've had enough. Tell me—"

But he was already talking, telling her what had happened, in his own disjointed way. "I've been thinking, lately, that I had to have it out with her."

"With Monica?"

"Yeah. The bitch. Had to draw the line on her, tell her I was through jumping through hoops for her. And then that proxy thing she's pulling, it was the final straw."

"Proxy?"

"She's been trying to take over the goddamn board."

"The board of Fortune Industries?"

"Right. It's too damn much. Got to stop her. Got to draw the line. So I went to her place."

"Tonight? You went to Monica Malone's tonight?"

"Yeah. I went there. To her mansion. Ever seen that place?"

"No, Dad."

He shook his head. "A monstrous exercise in bad taste, that place of Monica's. Fake as one of those two-bit costume dramas she used to star in. Fits her to a *T*." Jake shuddered.

"What happened there?"

"At Monica's?"

She nodded.

He looked away. "What happened at Monica's..." He pondered heavily for a moment, staring off toward the doors to the hall. And then his gaze was on Natalie again. "I...had it out with her. I tol' her I was through with it. Through with her and her tricks. Through with her demands. That she could tell it all, I didn't give a damn. I said I would be fighting her, every step of the way, from now on."

"Dad, what could she *tell?* You still haven't said."

He waved her words away with a weary hand. "Doesn't matter. The point is, she went wild." He blinked, rubbed his eyes.

"What do you mean, she went wild?"

He shook his head. "Drink. 'Nother drink."

Natalie held on to the arms of his chair. "Dad. I'm trying to understand. What happened?"

He groaned. "She fell."

"Fell? Dad. Dad look at me. Listen to me."

"I'm listening, Nat."

"Is she all right?"

He frowned. "All right?"

"You said Monica *fell....*"

He was still frowning. "What? No. No, never mind about that. We argued, that's all."

"You argued."

Her father nodded, then sighed heavily.

"And then what?"

He rubbed his eyes, dragged his hands down his face. "That's all. I saw it was getting nowhere. I'd said what I came to say. So I left. She was spitting threats at my back as I went out the door." He sighed, a sigh that turned into a hiccup. "Now, how 'bout another drink?"

"But what about your shoulder, Dad?"

"Huh?"

"What happened to your shoulder?"

He glanced at it. "Oh. That." He looked at Natalie, and blinked. "Don't know, Nat. Just don't know... But I can tell you for sure, I really need a drink..."

Natalie reached out and screwed the lid on the bottle. "No, Dad." She still didn't really know what was going on. But she knew as much as she was going to get out of him in his current condition. He'd had an argument with Monica Malone and he was upset about it. And right now, he needed rest. "It's time for bed." She stood and took him by both hands.

"Nat. C'mon..."

She almost smiled. He seemed so helpless. It was touching; and yet unreal. As a matter of fact, everything about tonight was beginning to seem unreal. "Let's go upstairs. You can clean up. I'll look at your shoulder, and—"

"I told you. Shoulder's nothing."

"You'll have a shower, and I'll look at your shoulder." She spoke in the firm tone she used on recalcitrant students. "And then you can go to bed."

He actually stuck out his lower lip. "I want a drink."

"No, Dad. You've had enough." She pulled on his hands. Surprisingly, he made no more protests. He staggered upright, falling against her as he got to his feet.

"Whoa, Nat. The world's spinning 'round a little faster than it should be...."

"Come on. It's okay." She wrapped his arm—the one on the uninjured side—over her shoulder.

"Where's my jacket?" he asked woozily.

She managed to reach behind him and snare it off the back of the chair. "Right here. I've got it."

He leaned against her. "You're a good girl, Natty. Good to your old dad. Wish your mother was one-tenth as understanding as you...."

"This way." She guided him toward the door.

By the time she got him up to his rooms, he'd turned cranky. But somehow, she managed to convince him to get out of his clothes and into the shower. While he bathed, she got his pajamas for him. But he wouldn't wear them. He told her through the bathroom door that he wasn't damn well ready for bed yet. So she passed him clean underwear, socks and a pair of slacks. When he had them on, she sat him down and took a look at the cut on his shoulder. It was superficial, as he'd kept insisting. She bandaged it and helped him into a polo shirt.

"Now enough, damn it," he insisted. "Stop fussing over me." He staggered over, scooped up his rumpled suit and torn shirt and stuffed them in the clothes hamper. "There. All cleaned up."

She did manage to convince him to swallow a couple of aspirin. And somehow she extracted a grudging promise that he'd leave the Scotch alone for the rest of the night. Feeling she'd done the best she could under the circumstances, she left him in the sitting room of the master suite, watching television.

Before going to her own room, Natalie returned to the foyer to get her bags, then stopped in the library once more and chose a novel to take to bed with her.

It was well after midnight when she finally settled under the covers in the blue room and opened the book to the first page.

In the master suite, Jake was watching the late late news on cable when he heard the update.

"As we reported when the news first broke, Monica Malone, the ever-youthful movie star and spokesmodel, has been found dead in her Minneapolis mansion...."

Jake blinked, his fogged mind refusing to take it in. He leaned forward, straining to catch every word.

"Though few details have been released, police are now admitting that it appears the actress was a victim of foul play...."

A long, tight moan escaped Jake. His shoulder throbbed. And he remembered all the parts of his encounter with Monica that he'd managed to keep from blurting out to Natalie.

"My son will replace you, Jake Fortune!" she'd shrieked at him. "Brandon will run Fortune Industries. I'll make that happen if it's the last thing I do."

Jake had thrown back his head and laughed at the very idea. He'd met Brandon Malone, Monica's adopted son, more than once. The man was his mother's errand boy, not CEO material by any stretch of the imagination.

"Don't you laugh at my son, you fatherless son of a bitch!" And then she'd come at him, wild-eyed, with a letter opener clutched in her hand. He'd put up his hands, but she'd still managed to cut through his jacket and his shirt and poke a hole in his shoulder.

He'd seen red. Grabbed for her. And all at once, they'd been tearing at each other, Monica screaming gutter words in his ear. He'd given her a good hard shove. And she'd fallen. Against that ridiculous marble fireplace with all those dancing, naked Cupids carved on it.

She'd hit her head. Been knocked out cold.

And he had stood there. Staring down at her. There had been blood in her hair. And she'd looked old. The witch was in her late sixties, maybe even seventy. But until then, every time Jake had been forced to deal with her, she'd always looked good.

But not then, not lying there with her legendary violet

eyes shut and her mouth hanging open and blood in her gorgeous blond hair.

Jake had thought, *Well, now Monica. Looks like you're not exactly ageless, after all.*

A minute later, she'd started moaning, coming to. Jake had helped her to a couch, even though what he really wanted to do was just to let her lie there on the floor.

The gutter language had been spilling out from between those red lips again. And he could see no point in hanging around. So he'd left.

Left her still very much alive and swearing to ruin him.

And that was all. The way it had happened. He was sure it was.

Wasn't it?

His gut roiled. His head throbbed.

Yeah, all right, he'd been drinking too much lately. But he wasn't that bad. He wasn't to the point where he had *blackouts* or anything.

Or was he?

No. Surely not. Especially not tonight. He'd watched himself, kept the drinks to a minimum, before going to visit Monica. He'd wanted a clear head.

"Once again," the announcer said, "Monica Malone, legendary star of the silver screen and the original Fortune's Face, is with us no more...."

Jake pulled himself to his feet. Once there, he reeled. His stomach pitched and tightened, sending a hot squirt of acid into his throat. His head pounded like drums in the jungle. He grabbed for the back of the sofa and managed to steady himself.

They would be after him. People must have seen him. Monica's household staff. People on the street, when he'd driven through her gates. And he'd *bled* on that letter opener, damn it. He'd left fingerprints all over everything. And Monica had fought with him. *Scratched* him. There'd be little bits of his skin under those long red nails of hers.

It was going to look bad. Worse than bad. With all the stuff they'd have on him, they wouldn't waste a millisecond following other leads.

Damn. He needed a clear head. Now, of all times. He needed to think this through.

He closed his eyes, tried to breathe slowly and evenly. But his heart was hammering, and his fogged mind seemed to be playing one theme song, over and over: *Go. Escape. Get away quick.*

One of his Porsches was out front, where he'd left it when he returned from Monica's. He wouldn't even have to call Edgar. He wouldn't have to disturb anyone at all....

Natalie woke from troubled dreams just as dawn lightened the sky. For a few moments, she imagined she might try to go back to sleep.

But she was wide awake, too troubled by the events of the night before to relax again right then. So she pulled on some leggings and a tunic and padded on bare feet down to the house's huge kitchen. The coffee, of course, was set up and ready to go. She set the dial to brew and then wandered over to a window that looked out on a side yard. The pot was just beginning to fill when the buzzer to the main gate out front rang.

Since one of the control consoles was on the wall nearby, she went to it and pushed the talk button. "Yes? Who is it, please?"

"Detectives Harbing and Rosczak, Minneapolis police. We'd like to speak with Jacob Fortune."

Natalie's heart seemed to stop—and then to rocket into

high gear. Her father seemed to have no end of problems lately. And now the *police* wanted to talk to him....

"Ma'am?" the voice demanded. "Are you there, ma'am? Will you please open the gates?"

She ordered her mind to think logically, and decided there was nothing to be gained by refusing them entry. "Yes. Of course. Come in." She pressed the button that would let them through.

The man on the other end was thanking her politely as she whirled and headed for the stairs.

Dread was an icy rock in her stomach when she pounded on her father's door. She waited. He didn't come. She put her ear to the door. She thought she heard the low drone of voices on the other side.

How long could it take him to get to the door? He'd been so drunk. Maybe he was out cold, dead to the world. But then who would be talking in there?

She tried the knob. It turned. "Dad?"

He wasn't in the sitting room, though she discovered the source of the voices she'd heard; he'd left the television on.

"Dad?" She went to the door of his bedroom.

He wasn't there, either. The spread on the bed was a wide, unwrinkled expanse.

She rubbed her tired eyes. *Think. Think...*

The library. Maybe he'd returned to the library to have some more of the Scotch he'd so solemnly promised to leave alone. Maybe he was passed out there now. She turned and sprinted for the stairs.

But when she got to the library, there was no sign of him. The room seemed undisturbed from the last time she'd seen it, the night before. She was staring at the half-empty bottle of Scotch and the short, thick crystal glass beside it when the front doorbell rang.

There was nothing to do but go and answer it.

When she reached the foyer, Mrs. Laughlin was already there. The housekeeper turned when she heard the whisper of Natalie's bare feet on the floor. "Shall I answer it, miss?"

Natalie squared her shoulders. "Yes, I suppose so."

Thirteen

At a little before eight, across the lake, Rick and Toby were just finishing up their breakfast when the house phone rang. Normally Natalie would be up by now, dressed in her exercise gear, jumping around to one of those fitness tapes of hers. She would have heard the ringing and answered on the upstairs line. But today the phone kept on ringing, which made Toby look up at Rick, his eyes questioning.

Rick gave his son a none-of-our-business shrug. He had heard Natalie leave last night, so he knew she wasn't there to answer her phone. The machine on the counter not far away would handle it.

After the fourth ring, they were treated to Natalie's voice, asking her caller to please leave a message. And then they heard Erica.

"Natalie? Natalie, please. Pick up." A pause. "Natalie? I mean it. This is urgent...."

Toby's brows drew together. "Daddy?" The sound was thready and didn't have much volume, but the single word seemed to have a thousand meanings:

Something's wrong. You have to answer. Fix things, Daddy. Make things right....

"Natalie. Oh, Nat. *Please...*"

Rick couldn't stand the agitation in Erica Fortune's voice— not to mention his son's trusting, worried eyes on him. He stood.

On the other end of the phone line, Erica sighed. "All right. I can see that you're not—"

Rick picked up the phone before she could finish. "Hello, Mrs. Fortune. This is—"

"Rick? Is that you, Rick?"

"Yes, it's me."

"Oh, thank God. I must speak with Natalie. Is she there?"

"I'm afraid not."

"Do you know where she is, then?"

He hesitated, thinking of the night before, reluctant to reveal anything that Natalie wouldn't want her mother to know.

"Rick?"

"She went over to the estate last night."

"She's been at the estate...all night?"

He couldn't think of anything to tell her but the truth. "She drove over after ten."

"After ten. Did she happen to see her father, then?"

"I wouldn't know. I haven't spoken with her since she left." Toby was still looking at him. He turned his back to the boy and lowered his voice. "Mrs. Fortune, what is going on?"

There was a silence on the line. Then Erica said, "I shouldn't burden you with this. It has nothing to do with you."

"I'd like to help, if I can."

Erica hesitated another long moment before admitting, "It's Jake."

"Your husband?"

"Yes. The police have called here at my house, looking for him. They said they've already been to the estate. And that he wasn't there. Of course, I immediately contacted Sterling Foster, who's handled our family's legal matters for years."

"Yes, I've met Sterling."

"He said he would deal with it. But I can't settle down. I'm simply frantic. I really have been trying not to bother Nat. I understand she has her own life. But I thought, if I could just speak with her, I'd feel a little better. She always calms me down."

"I understand."

"And what you've just told me makes it worse. She must have been there, this morning, when the police—"

"Stay calm, Mrs. Fortune. Explain to me why the police would want to talk to your husband."

"Oh, God..."

"Take it slow. It's okay."

"I know, I know. They...they want to talk to him about his whereabouts last night."

"Why?"

"Because somebody killed Monica Malone last night. And the authorities believe..." She couldn't quite bring herself to finish.

"I understand." He wished he didn't. But he'd heard enough about the situation to see how Jake Fortune might be a suspect, if someone had eliminated Monica Malone.

"My husband is not a murderer. But where is he? Where can he be?"

"Mrs. Fortune—"

"Oh, I shouldn't have burdened you with all of this."

"It's all right."

"Forgive me."

"Of course."

"I will call Natalie now, over at the estate. I'll feel better, after I talk to her."

He thought of Natalie, all alone on the other side of

the lake, dealing with the police, probably going nuts worrying about her father. Even after the ugly way it had ended between them last night, he couldn't help wondering who was going to make *her* feel better.

Erica was still talking. "In the meantime, if she should show up there, would you have her call me, right away?"

"Certainly."

"Goodbye, then." The line went dead.

Rick turned to put the phone in its cradle and found that his son was still watching him.

Toby said another word. "Nat'lie?"

Rick swiftly reassured him. "She's all right. She's fine. That was about...something else."

Toby didn't have to say, *What else?* It was written all over his worried little face.

How in the hell did a man ease a child's mind without actually telling him anything? Rick did his best. "It's just some...family problems, that's all. It's nothing for us to worry about."

Toby's frown didn't deepen so much as become more set.

"Really, Toby. There's nothing we can do."

Toby didn't look convinced. He just sat very still, looking at his father and continuing to frown. And then the damn dog, who'd been snoozing on the rug a few feet away, suddenly lifted his giant head and let out a whine. A worried-sounding whine. The dog looked at Rick. It was a reproachful look.

"Cut it out," Rick said. But the dog's soft brown gaze didn't waver.

Rick looked away—and there was Toby, frowning. Rick looked back at the dog, who now seemed to be frowning, too. He tried to remember that *he* was the boss here. And that his judgment was much more developed than that of a five-year-old or a Saint Bernard—as if a dog could have the vaguest idea of what was going on here, anyway.

"She won't want us to interfere."

The boy and the dog went on looking at him.

"She's not in any danger, I promise you."

They remained unconvinced.

Rick threw up his hands. "All right, damn it. We'll go."

They took the ski boat; it was fast, and going across the lake was much quicker than driving the rambling shore road would have been. Rick had planned to leave the dog behind, but the animal jumped in the boat before he could be told to stay. And then, when he was in there, he looked as if he wouldn't be easy to remove.

"I suppose you ride in this thing all the time."

The dog only gazed at him.

"You'd better sit still."

The dog panted. To Rick, he looked smug.

"All right, fine. You can go."

Rick helped Toby into a life jacket, then admonished him to sit still, just as he had the dog. Then, after a couple of false tries, he got the thing started and out of the boathouse. They took off across the lake.

The Fortune mansion wasn't that hard to find. Natalie had pointed it out to Rick the day they arrived at the farmhouse. And Rick and Toby had spotted it more than once during the many days they spent on the lake. Also, it was almost a direct shot across from the farmhouse.

Thus, they were pulling up to the Fortune dock within ten minutes of leaving the boathouse. Rick tied the line to a piling and helped Toby out. Bernie had already leapt out and was waiting for them on the shore.

A sweeping lawn led up to the back of the house, where it met a wide stone terrace rimmed by a low wall. Looking out onto the terrace were a set of graceful French doors. Rick stared up at the jewellike glass of the doors and wondered how likely it was that there would be anyone in the room beyond to answer if he knocked.

No, it would be wiser to go around front and ring the bell.

"This way," he said to his son and the dog, who fell right in step with him.

It was a big house, and it took several minutes to get around to the other side of it, but they managed. Soon enough, they were standing in the cavelike recessed porch beneath the front portico. Rick rang the bell.

They didn't have to wait long before a serious-looking gray-haired woman answered. She was frowning. "Yes?"

"I'm Rick Dalton, Natalie Fortune's tenant at the farmhouse across the lake. I believe she came here last night, and I'd like to speak with her, please."

The woman looked from the dog to the child and then back at Rick. "Pardon me, but how did you get through the gate?"

"We came across the lake."

"Ah." The woman's frown disappeared, but she didn't go so far as to crack a smile. "Wait right here. I'll check with Ms. Fortune."

"Thanks."

She was careful to close the door on them before she turned away.

His son and the dog were looking at him. He gave them what he hoped was a reassuring, everything's-under-control kind of smile.

The door opened again. "She says she'll see you."

The maid sighed. "Including the dog. This way." The maid led them through the huge entryway. Bernie's paws tapped time on the gleaming floors as they walked down a hall that finally brought them to a high-ceilinged living room with a bank of French doors along one wall. Rick recognized those doors. They led out to that flagstone terrace he'd seen a while ago from outside.

The richly furnished room was spacious enough to contain several conversation groups of silk-upholstered furniture. Natalie sat alone on a sofa in one of those groups, looking lost and numb. Toby and Bernie made a beeline to her side.

The maid asked, "Will there be anything else, miss?"

"No. Thank you. That's all."

The maid left, and Natalie turned her full attention on Toby and the dog. "Oh." She sounded sad and grateful and very near to tears. "Oh, hi…"

Rick watched, his heart doing something traitorous inside his chest, as she opened her arms and Toby went into them. The minute she'd hugged Toby, she reached for the dog, giving him the same enthusiastic embrace the boy had received.

When she released the dog, she sat back and looked at Rick. "You shouldn't have come." Her tone was careful, subdued.

"We were worried."

Her slim shoulders lifted in a shrug of pure weariness. "My mother called a little while ago. She said she'd told you…the problem."

"Yes."

She stared at him rather vacantly for a moment. Then she shook herself. "Oh, Rick…I'm not sure what to do next.…"

The boy and the dog, sensing her distress but not understanding it, sought to give comfort. Toby patted her arm. The dog swiped at her hand with his big wet tongue.

Rick struggled over how much he could afford to say with impressionable ears listening in. "Your mother said that your father has disappeared."

"Yes. He's gone. Somewhere... I don't know where, really. I've been trying to reach Sterling. You remember Sterling?"

"Yes, I remember."

"I called his house, and he was out. So the best I could do was to leave him a message."

"Your mother said she already spoke with him."

"Yes. But there are some...some things I must discuss with him. Some things my mother isn't aware of."

"What things?"

She glanced at Toby. Rick understood. They would have to find another opportunity to carry this conversation further.

"Look," Rick said. "I think you should come with us. Back home."

She blinked. "Home." All that had happened between them last night was there in her eyes. "But I—"

He didn't wait for her excuses. "Did you bring a suitcase?"

"Yes, a small one. It's up in my room. But, really, Rick—"

"Get it." He spared a glance for her bare feet. "And put on some shoes. We're leaving."

"But I have to talk to Sterling—"

"You can call him from the farmhouse."

"Do you really think my going back there is wise?"

He looked at her levelly. "You'll be happier at home. You know it. This place is too big and too empty for you to stay here alone right now."

"But we..." She cast a glance at Toby, and plainly didn't know how to finish.

Rick did it for her, vaguely enough that he hoped his son wouldn't really know what he was talking about. "Natalie, last night we came to an agreement about where we stand with each other. As far as I'm concerned, nothing on that level has changed. But right now, you're in trouble, and you could use a helping hand. I'm offering mine. Maybe you just ought to take it and stop reading a thousand different meanings into everything I do."

She searched his face. And then she nodded. "I'll get my things."

Natalie drove her car back around the lake. Rick, Toby and Bernie returned the way they'd come, in the ski boat.

Natalie knew Rick had been right when she pulled into the gravel drive and looked up at the comfortable wooden house. She belonged here, not in the empty mansion across the lake.

Inside, Rick, Toby and Bernie were already waiting for her. Natalie called Sterling's house again, but was told he was out. She left a second message, asking that he call her immediately at the farmhouse.

When she hung up, all she wanted to do was pace the floor. But Rick set some toast in front of her.

"Eat." He poured her a cup of coffee.

"I'm not hungry."

"Eat."

So she doggedly picked up a wedge of toast and stuck the corner in her mouth.

At last, around nine-fifteen, Sterling called back. He promised he'd be right over. Thirty-one minutes later, the lawyer was knocking on the front door.

Rick had a video of *The Lion King*. He settled Toby

in the great room with Bernie, to watch it. The adults retreated to the front parlor.

Natalie sat on the sofa, and Sterling took one of the wing chairs. Rick stayed on his feet, near Natalie. He didn't miss the measuring glances that Sterling sent his way, and he fully expected the old gentleman to find some tactful way to ask him to leave the room.

But all Sterling said was "It appears that Natalie trusts you." Then the white-haired lawyer looked at Natalie, who gave him a quick nod. "All right, then. Let's proceed."

In a low, tight voice, Natalie told of the condition she'd found her father in the night before.

"You say his shirt was torn, and blood-spotted at the shoulder?"

She nodded. "Somehow, he must have cut himself."

"Is that what he told you?"

"No." She glanced away, and then back. "He didn't tell me anything, really. He was…incoherent. I told him he'd had enough to drink and coaxed him up to his room."

"And that's all?"

"I looked at his shoulder. The wound was minor. I cleaned it and put a bandage on it."

"And then?"

"I left him alone." Natalie sighed and rubbed at her temples. Rick, still standing close, couldn't stop himself wishing he could make this all easier for her. Involuntarily his hand went out, but he caught himself just in time and dropped it to his side.

Sterling instructed, "Now tell me about what happened when you talked to the police."

Natalie launched into a story of how two detectives

from the Minneapolis police had rung the bell at the front gate at six-thirty that morning.

"Did they have a warrant?"

"I don't think so. They never mentioned one. And I never asked them for one. I thought it would be foolish to refuse to cooperate with them."

"Wise move. So you let them in...."

"Yes. I opened the gate from the kitchen control panel, and then I ran up to Dad's rooms to tell him they were there." Natalie drew in a breath and let it out slowly. "He wasn't in his rooms. The television in the sitting room was still on, and his bed looked untouched. I went down and checked in the library, where I'd found him the night before. He wasn't there, either."

"What happened next?"

"The detectives were at the door by then. There's a new housekeeper at the estate. She let them in. They asked if they could look around, and I said they could. Then they asked me about what had happened last night. I told them what I've just told you. After they finally went away, I realized that Dad must have left in the black sports car—it had been in front of the house last night when I first arrived, around eleven."

"How much did you tell the detectives about what Jake said to you in the library?"

Natalie blinked, then looked toward the front windows. "Nothing." She met Sterling's eyes again. "Just what I told you. That he'd been drinking and that he was incoherent. I said I had helped him up to the master suite and left him watching television. They asked me if I'd seen anything odd in his behavior, if he'd said anything unusual, if he'd happened to mention Monica Malone. And I, um..."

The distress in her voice had Rick clenching his fists at his sides.

Sterling leaned forward in his chair. "Natalie. It's all right. Tell me exactly what you said."

"I…" Her voice was very small. "Sterling, he did mention something. About Monica Malone blackmailing him. About going to see her earlier in the evening. About having an argument with her. But it really was garbled."

"Did you tell that to the police?"

She looked at Sterling for a moment, then wrapped her arms around herself and shivered a little, though it wasn't cold at all in the parlor.

"Natalie…" Sterling prodded.

And then she lifted her chin. "No. I didn't tell that to the police. I said that he'd been incoherent. That I couldn't make sense of anything he said."

"I see."

"I know it was wrong, that in a way I lied to them, by omission. But I'd probably do it all over again. I've been…confused about a lot of things lately. But last night, when I saw Dad the way he was, it came very clear to me that I'm a Fortune, first and foremost. I'm a Fortune. And when you're a Fortune, you stick by your own."

Sterling studied her face. Then he nodded. "I understand. And, unhappily for Jake, from what I'm piecing together here, they're going to have a mountain of evidence against him. Whatever he said to you last night probably isn't going to matter much, anyway—as long as what you've told me is all of it."

"What do you mean?"

Sterling's gaze was ice-blue now. "I mean, if he said more, if he, perhaps, actually confessed to you that he did more than just argue with the Malone woman, you should tell me right now."

Natalie leapt to her father's defense. "No, Sterling. He never said anything like that. He said they argued. And he muttered something about her falling. But then, when I tried to get him to explain, he said that she was all right. That they'd argued and he'd left and that was all there was to it."

"Did he say what Monica Malone was blackmailing him with?"

"No. I asked several times. But he never would tell me."

"Have you heard the news or read the papers this morning?"

Natalie gave a shrill little laugh. "I've been pretty busy this morning, Sterling."

That did it for Rick. He had to reach out. He laid a hand on her shoulder. She stiffened and looked up at him.

"Easy," he said, and smiled at her. She didn't smile back, but he felt her relax a little. Then he looked at Sterling. "What are you getting at?"

"It's all over the morning papers. Monica was stabbed several times in the chest with a letter opener."

Natalie let out a small cry of distress. "Oh, no..."

Sterling stood. "Natalie, you said Jake's shoulder was injured."

"But he wouldn't tell me how it got that way. He just looked at it and shrugged and said he didn't remember. Sterling, he was really drunk. It was so hard to make sense of what he said."

"All right. But are you sure that's all? Are you sure there's nothing else you think I should know?"

She looked up at the lawyer, her big eyes full of worry and sorrow. "No. That's all. That's everything."

"Then I have to be going. There's much to do. If any more detectives should come around asking questions, insist that your lawyer be present before you say anything. And then give me a call."

"Yes, I'll do that. I promise."

The older man smiled at Rick. "Take good care of her."

Rick answered without hesitation. "I will."

Natalie looked from Sterling to Rick and then back to Sterling. "No," she said. "You don't understand...."

"What?" Sterling asked, lifting one thick silver brow.

And then Natalie was blushing. "Nothing. Never mind. I'll walk you to the door."

Rick stayed where he was as Natalie saw Sterling out.

At the door, Natalie took Sterling's arm. "If you hear anything, will you let me know?"

He patted her hand. "Of course I will."

Sterling called Kate to give her an update as soon as he reached his house. Earlier that morning, when he received Erica's call, he had rushed to Kate's penthouse, so they'd already shared an hour-long conference about the situation. She had sent him back to his place with instructions to stay put, in case Jake called him.

"Have you heard from Jake?" she asked, as soon as she heard his voice.

"No. Not yet. But I've been to see Natalie."

"Natalie? What for?"

Swiftly he told her all Natalie had said.

Kate sighed. "It doesn't look good."

"No, it doesn't. Not at all." He cast about for something to lift her spirits a little. "But I think you were right about the architect and Natalie."

He heard her breath hitch. "What? Tell me."

"I can't be sure. It's only a hunch."

"A hunch will do fine."

"He was right there beside her every minute I was in the house, up until she walked me to the door."

"Yes?"

"And he couldn't help reaching out—when the going got rough for her."

"Good. Very good." She was quiet. "Call me. The minute you hear anything."

"You know I will."

Back at the farmhouse, Natalie insisted on reading the newspaper story about Monica's death. What Sterling had told her seemed even worse in black and white.

After that, they waited in an agony of impatience for news. An hour later, Sterling called.

"Natalie, I've just received a call from your father."

Natalie clutched the phone in fingers that felt suddenly numb. "How is he? Is he all right?"

"He's...fine." Natalie didn't like the way he hesitated over the word, but he didn't give her time to ask him why. "I must leave now. To handle the situation. Do you understand?"

She didn't, really, but she heard herself saying, "Yes," anyway.

"Will you call your mother for me and tell her that Jake's all right?"

"Yes, of course. But, Sterling—"

"I really must go now." And the line went dead.

Rick took the phone from her nerveless fingers. "What's happened?"

She looked at him, gaining strength from the steadiness of his gaze. "I'm not sure. Apparently my father has contacted Sterling. And Sterling's planning to go to him now.''

"That's good news, isn't it?"

Natalie shrugged helplessly. "How can I tell? He wouldn't say any more. He was in such a hurry."

"Natalie, I think Sterling's a very competent man."

"Yes, yes, I know." She shook herself. "He asked me to call my mother. I should do that now."

"Do you want me to do it for you?"

Natalie gaped at him. And not because he'd offered. But because she was so tempted to say yes.

She cleared her throat. "No. No, I'll do it."

He handed her back the phone, pressed the plunger to disconnect from Sterling's call and then ran a finger down her auto-dial list. When he got to her mother's name, he pushed the button beside it.

"Hello, this is Erica Fortune."

"Mother. It's Natalie."

"Oh, Nat." The sweet, brittle voice brimmed with gratitude. "I've just been going crazy here. I'm so glad you've called."

"I have news."

Her mother sucked in a quick breath. "Yes?"

Rick was making signals at her. She put her hand over the receiver. "What?"

"Invite her to come over here," he said. "I'll bet she's going nuts all alone at her house."

She blinked and wondered whether somehow Rick Dalton knew her mother better than she did.

"Natalie? Natalie, are you there?"

"Um, yes, Mom. I'm here. Listen. Why don't you come on over? To my house. And we'll talk about all of this."

Erica jumped at the invitation. "I'll be right there."

When her mother arrived, Natalie took her upstairs, where Toby wouldn't hear, and told her the news Sterling had given her.

"But where *is* Jake?" Erica wanted to know.

"I don't know, Mother. Sterling just asked me to call you and tell you that he was all right."

"'All right.' What does that mean?"

"I've been wondering the same thing."

When they came downstairs, Rick had lunch made. Toby had set four places.

"Eat with us," Rick said to Erica.

So they all sat down and ate the soup and sandwiches Rick had prepared. It was a silent meal. In the quiet, Natalie couldn't help but think of Rick and how terrific he was being about everything.

Once, he looked up from his bowl of soup and gave her a quick, encouraging smile. Her heart headed straight for meltdown.

She quickly lowered her gaze to her own bowl as all the awful things she'd said to him last night scrolled through her brain. She'd been telling herself for weeks that he was troubled and needy and would only use her if she let him get close. But, really, who was the needy one here? More and more, she was finding out that it certainly wasn't Rick.

"Eat, Nat'lie," Toby said.

Natalie heard her mother's soft intake of breath; Erica knew that Toby had been mute for months.

Toby smiled. "It's good for you."

Natalie smiled back at the boy as she picked up her spoon and dipped it into the soup.

Erica took her leave soon after they finished eating. But right after she left, the phone started ringing.

Natalie's sisters and her brother all called; so did Aunt

Lindsay and Aunt Rebecca. They'd heard the news and wanted to know whether Natalie could tell them anything more than they'd read in the papers. Natalie reported most of what she knew—leaving out what Jake had said the night before and never mentioning Jake's shoulder wound or the torn, bloody shirt he'd been wearing when she found him in the library.

Later in the afternoon, Rick said he had to run into Travistown to pick up a carton of milk; lately Toby was drinking the stuff by the gallon, it seemed. He invited Natalie, but she was reluctant to leave the phone, in case there might be more news about her father.

"But maybe you could just let Toby stay here with me," she suggested hopefully. "I could use the company."

So Rick went off by himself, promising to return in no time at all.

Natalie's upstairs phone was cordless, so she took it out on the back lawn with her and sat in a folding chair under a tree, watching as Toby threw a stick for Bernie. After a while, Toby grew bored with that game. He went back in the house and came out again toting a plastic ball and bat. He marched over to Natalie.

"Play ball," he said.

In spite of all the worries that preyed on her mind, Natalie couldn't say no to those blue eyes that were just like Rick's and that adorable smile that was Toby's alone. She followed him out into the sun and pitched to him for a while. He managed to hit about one in ten balls.

"You need a demonstration of batting technique," she told him.

He looked skeptical.

"Here." She held out the ball. "You pitch to me."

She took the bat and he took the ball. But then it turned

out that he needed as much work on his pitching as he needed on his batting. So she set down the bat and went to him and guided him through the moves of pitching underhand.

After ten minutes of practice, he could throw well enough that if she scrambled, she had a chance of getting a hit every now and then.

"Your dad is gonna be impressed," she told him.

Toby puffed out his skinny chest and looked very proud.

And then, right after that, on the next pitch, he threw a beauty. It floated right toward her plastic bat. She swung at it, smooth and gloriously.

And she connected—boy, did she connect.

All three of them, the boy, the dog and the woman, stood watching with their mouths open as the plastic ball sailed up—and right over the roof of the house.

They heard it bounce on the other side.

Natalie looked at Toby. "C'mon. Let's get it." And they took off at a run.

In the front yard, they discovered that the ball was stuck in a rain gutter of the second-floor roof.

"Aw, cheez," Toby muttered.

"Whattaya mean, 'Aw, cheez'?" Natalie demanded. "I know what you're thinking. You're thinking that you're going to have to wait until your dad gets home to get that ball, aren't you?"

Solemnly Toby nodded.

"Because you think that a kid and a woman and a dog can't manage something like getting a ball down off a roof on their own, don't you? You think they have to have a *man* around to do something like that, right?"

Toby nodded again.

"Wrong."

Toby grinned.

"Just you watch."

So Toby and Bernie watched as Natalie got her aluminum ladder from the garage and propped it against the roof of the porch. She was careful to test it for stability before she climbed it.

It wasn't far at all to the skirtlike porch roof. And from there, she carefully shuffled her way up the roof to the windows and the wall of the second story. Once there, she grabbed the storm drain with one hand—but gently, just for security. And she fished out the plastic ball with the other. Then she turned and held it up in triumph.

Toby clapped appreciatively, and Bernie even let out a bark of admiration. Natalie felt very pleased with herself.

She looked up at the sky and saw how blue and clear it was. And she felt good for the first time that day.

Now all she had to do was get back down the ladder before Rick got home and yelled at her for not waiting and letting him handle it.

She started toward the ladder, smiling, imagining how pleased he'd be when he heard the kind of progress Toby was making with his plastic ball and bat. Why, with a few weeks of constant practice, Toby could turn out to be one fine little slugger. Maybe, now that she thought about it, she wouldn't say anything to Rick. She'd wait awhile, till she'd had more time to practice with Toby, and then...

She stopped herself in midthought. What was the matter with her? She was thinking of Rick and his son as if they were a permanent part of her life.

Which they weren't. And never would be.

She had ruined any chance of that last night.

Natalie knew at that moment what a fool she'd really been. And because she was thinking more about Rick than about watching her footing, she tripped.

Fourteen

Natalie heard Toby's shout of fear as she slid down the slope of the porch roof and right off the edge. She managed to give a little push when she flew out into thin air, and that sent her beyond the hedge that grew thick and scratchy close to the porch railing. She landed on the grass.

Unfortunately, she somehow got her left leg caught under her at an odd angle. She heard a distinct snapping sound.

With a little groan, she rolled onto her back, then lifted up on an elbow and looked down at her leg. It was still straight. But it didn't feel right. Not right at all. She reached out for it, to rub the place where it had started to throb a little, on the shin right below her knee. The moment she touched it, pain shot through her, hot and fierce. She grunted and leaned back on her hands, which caused another burning stab of pain.

She felt Bernie's warm breath on her neck. The dog whined and nuzzled her.

"Nat'lie?" Toby was right there beside her, fear and concern written all over his small face.

She hastened to reassure him. "I'm okay. I hurt my leg, that's all." Miraculously, she still held the plastic ball in her hand. "Here you go." She handed it to Toby.

He looked down at it, and then up at her once more.

She gave him the best grin she could come up with,

under the circumstances. "And now, how about if you go back around to the other side of the house and get my phone for me? It's on that little table beside where I was sitting."

He dropped his ball and took off at a run.

He was at her side again in about a minute. He handed her the phone, and she dialed 911, gave her address and asked for an ambulance. When she was finished, she shifted a little, considering the idea of trying to drag herself into the house. But she gave that thought up right away. The pain in her leg was manageable, as long as she remained still. "I think I'll just lie here, all right? For a little bit." Her leg screaming in protest, she lowered herself back onto the grass.

Toby knelt beside her. His small hand smoothed her hair. "Don't be 'fraid. Daddy will come."

Natalie said nothing, only forced another smile for him. Toby stroked her hair, as Bernie stretched out on her other side, big and warm and solid. Natalie stared up at the blue bowl of the sky and made herself breathe evenly.

She glanced at Toby. "So much for that cruise."

His expression turned curious. "Cruise?"

"I was going to fly far away on Monday, and then get on a big boat and go traveling to many exotic lands."

"Exotic?"

"That's like strange and different."

Toby patted her shoulder. "You better just stay here."

"Yes. Yes, I think I'd better. I think going on a cruise right now would be bad timing, all the way around."

The decision made, she took Toby's small hand and held it, closing her eyes with a sigh.

"What's happened here?"

Natalie opened her eyes to see Rick standing over her.

"Nat'lie's hurted," Toby said.

"It's my leg," she explained, feeling sheepish. "I think I broke it."

Rick knelt and touched her leg. Natalie bit back a moan. Toby held her hand tight.

"I'm not going to ask how this happened," Rick said.

"Good." It sounded more like a grunt of pain than a word.

Rick went on, "I don't trust myself to move you. I'm going in and calling an ambulance."

She felt for the phone on the lawn right beside her, and held it up with a proud grimace. "I did that already."

He took the phone from her. "Okay, then. All we have to do is wait."

"I can do that." She tried to sit up again. Her leg throbbed harder than before. With a whimper she couldn't quite hold back, she sank to the grass again. "I think."

When the ambulance arrived, Rick insisted on going to the hospital, too. He went upstairs, put Natalie's phone in its recharging base and got a change of clothes for her, since one of the EMTs had told him they would probably end up having to cut her leggings off her. Then he took Toby and followed the ambulance in his car. Only Bernie stayed at home, staring after them longingly as they headed away down the drive.

The hospital where the ambulance took Natalie was much smaller than Minneapolis General, where her aunt Lindsay was a resident pediatrician. The emergency room staff consisted of one doctor and one nurse, both of whom had their hands full with other patients when Natalie arrived. It quickly became obvious that it would be a while before Natalie's leg could be x-rayed and set.

More than once, as they waited, Natalie urged Rick to take Toby on home.

"There's no reason you have to hang around here with me," she argued. "I can call my mother and she'll be here in a flash."

"Your mother's already upset enough as is," Rick replied, which was just what Natalie had been thinking herself. "Why worry her any more? We'll call her when everything's taken care of and you're back at home."

His argument made sense, but still she felt guilty about making him and Toby wait around.

She tried another tactic. "Something might come up about my father. If you were home, you could handle it."

He looked at her with frank skepticism. "Come on. The most that's going to happen at home is that someone will call with more information on the situation. They'll leave a message. And we'll follow up when we get back. Let it go. I'm not leaving until you can come with me."

She looked in his eyes and wished she could throw her arms around him and tell him how wonderful he was. But that would be completely out of line, and she knew it. She sighed and stopped arguing. She didn't feel like arguing, anyway. They'd given her a shot to kill the pain while she waited. And she was feeling halfway between numb and euphoric. In no condition for arguing at all.

"We'll stay." Rick made his point one more time, softly, holding her gaze. "Say, 'thank you.'"

So she did.

When they finally left for home early in the evening, Natalie's leg was protected by a lightweight cast, which the doctor had assured her would be much more comfortable than the old-fashioned kind. She also checked out with a pair of crutches and a big bottle of pain pills.

"You were lucky," the doctor told her. "It's just a

hairline fracture of the tibia. Keep it elevated as much as possible, and stay off it if you can. You'll be your old self again in six weeks or so.''

They gave her another shot before she departed, so the ride home was quite pleasant. She sat in the back, with her leg stretched along the seat, feeling peaceful and dreamy and not really all there.

At home, there were several messages on Natalie's answering machine. Most were from family members, wanting to know whether Natalie had heard anything new about Jake. Two were from reporters, asking Natalie to please call them back. There was nothing from Sterling. Natalie called the members of her family, ignored the reporters and hoped that her father was still "all right." She decided not to call Erica after all. There was really no reason to bother her right now. Natalie's mother had enough on her mind.

Since it was so much trouble for her to get up and down the stairs, Rick decided she would take over his room and he would sleep in a spare room on the second floor.

"Rick, I can't take your room."

"Shh... Don't argue. You're in no condition to argue, and you know it."

So Natalie watched, feeling useless and burdensome, as Rick changed the sheets for her, carried some of his things upstairs and brought hers down. Then he went out to the kitchen and cooked them all some dinner. When she hobbled in and offered to help, he told her to go put her leg up, he was managing just fine.

They had to talk, she decided as he was cleaning up the kitchen all by himself. So as soon as Toby was in bed, she gobbled down a couple of painkillers and limped to the great room on her new crutches.

"Rick, I'd like to talk to you."

He was sitting on the sofa with his *Newsweek* on his lap. The television was on with the sound low. They'd been leaving it that way, on the chance that they might catch any late-breaking news about Monica Malone's death or about Jake. So far, there had been nothing they didn't already know.

Rick picked up the remote and turned the sound down all the way. Then he tossed the magazine onto the coffee table and stood. "You're supposed to keep that leg up."

"I'm fine."

He shoved an ottoman in front of an easy chair and grabbed some throw pillows to put on top. "Come on. Get over here."

She stumped to the chair. When she got there, he was waiting to help her down into it. "Thanks, but I can manage."

"Have it your way." He sounded exasperated, but he did step back, returning to the couch, where he sat down again, so easily and so gracefully that she was green with envy.

Now it was her turn to sit. She knew it wouldn't be pretty. And it wasn't. With more grunting and groaning than could possibly be considered attractive, she dropped into the chair, laid her crutches on the floor at her side and hoisted her aching leg onto the ottoman and its pile of pillows.

"All right," he said when she was finally settled. "Let's *talk*." The way he stressed the word reminded her of the other talks they'd had since he came to stay at the farmhouse. There had been the talk when she told him she would never become involved with him. The talk when he asked her whether they could be "friendly." And, of course, the talk last night, when she accused him of having all kinds of despicable motives for making love to her, until he finally agreed with her that what they'd shared had been a big mistake.

"Well?" He lifted an eyebrow at her.

She ordered her tired, drugged mind to stay in the now. "Yes. All right."

How to begin? She dragged in a breath and forged ahead. "This just isn't fair to you."

He let a beat elapse before asking, "What isn't fair?"

"You're spending all of your time taking care of me."

"We're managing."

"But it's not right. You came here to be with Toby, not to play nursemaid to your landlady."

He yawned.

Irritation sizzled through her. "I'm sorry. Am I keeping you awake?"

"It's late." He stood and stretched, looking so handsome and strong and *masculine* that, even with her incessantly throbbing leg and her mind fogged with pain medicine, she remembered last night. The way he had looked at her, the way he had touched her, how beautifully male he was when he was naked, and how it had felt when he—

She closed her eyes tight to make the memories go away.

"Natalie, you really need sleep. Let me help you to bed."

She opened her eyes. He was standing right over her.

"I'm trying to talk to you."

"Fine." He hooked his fingers in the belt loops of his jeans. "Spit it out, then."

She stuck out her chin. "All right. I will. I think I should go and stay at my mother's."

He grunted. "Do you *want* to go and stay at your mother's?"

Now why did he have to put it that way?

"I didn't think so." His half smile was annoyingly smug.

She felt pitiful and incompetent and utterly miserable. "I'm a capable woman." It didn't sound convincing.

"I know you are." His tone was gentler. "It's a rough time, that's all. You've just had one too many things to deal with in the past few days." He gave her a smile that turned her insides to mush. "Now, come on. Bedtime." He scooped up her crutches, then held out a hand to help her up.

She stared at that hand. "Rick."

"What?"

"I'm sorry." He dropped his hand and backed away a step. She made herself raise her glance to his face. Her throat closed up. She coughed to relax it. "I'm sorry for all those awful things I said to you last night. I...I was confused. And I was wrong. It's obvious from...all you've done for me and my family today that you can take care of Toby just fine without any help from me."

He kept on watching her. She had no idea in the world what he might be thinking.

She made herself continue. "And Sterling insisted on having you checked out, before you moved in here. His people are *very* thorough, I promise you. Which means that if you'd wanted an introduction to one of the Fortune companies, or if you'd had any money problems, they would have found out. So, I really do realize that I was way out of line. And I can't take back what I said. I can only say that I honestly regret it and hope you will consider accepting my apology." She swallowed. "Please."

Rick went on looking at her. When about a century

had passed without him saying anything, she couldn't take it anymore.

"All right. I get it. Apology not accepted." She started to push herself out of the chair. He stepped closer again, and she dropped back with a small gasp. "What?"

His eyes were like a pair of laser beams; they cut right to the center of her.

"What? Say it. Please."

"All right. I accept your apology. Now, come on. It's time for bed."

Fifteen minutes later, she was lying in Rick's bed, wearing an extralarge T-shirt for a nightgown. Her leg, elevated in a nest of pillows, pulsed dully. But she wasn't really thinking about her leg.

She was thinking about her father, wondering where he could be, praying that he was going to come through all the awful things that were happening to him.

And she was admitting again how totally she'd blown it with Rick. He'd been nothing short of wonderful today. She might as well be honest with herself; about now, she would trade her trust fund for another chance with him.

But he'd been so...unreadable, when she stumbled through that apology. Probably because he was still as certain as he'd been last night that it was over between them. And really, how could she blame him if that was how he felt? She'd insisted from the first that she wouldn't get involved with him, so he was only giving her what she'd claimed to want all along.

Oh, but he'd been so gentle when he helped her down the hall to this room she'd stolen from him. Her leg had felt like a lead weight; she'd looked none too graceful, she knew it, stumbling along. And she could have used a bath. She wasn't dirty, exactly. But she certainly wasn't fresh and clean-smelling, either. However, with her leg in a cast, a bath was going to be an adventure—one she hadn't been up to tackling that night. Her hair felt stringy, ready for a good shampoo. The bald truth was, she'd had all the sexual allure of an old rag.

But still, she hadn't been able to stop herself thinking how strong his arms felt. She'd even dared to imagine how piercingly sweet it would be if he would only kiss her once. Not a passionate kiss, even. Just a quick, gentle good-night kiss.

But he hadn't. She'd been burning up with awareness of him, and he'd treated her like just what she was: a bedraggled woman with a newly broken leg who needed help getting around.

Natalie let out a long, sorry sigh.

She really had to face facts. Rick Dalton was a good, generous man, doing what he could for another human being during a difficult time. He was through with her romantically. And the sooner she accepted that, the better off she'd be.

The phone rang very late. In her eagerness to apologize to Rick and in her confusion afterward, when he insisted on helping her to bed, Natalie had forgotten to do anything about plugging a phone into the line in the downstairs bedroom.

But Rick, as usual, took care of the problem. He got up and crossed the landing to her upstairs rooms and answered it for her. She had managed to drag herself out to the bottom of the stairs when he emerged with her remote phone in his hand. He was wearing black sweatpants and nothing else. She tried not to look at his gorgeous bare chest as he took the stairs two at a time to reach her side.

He put his hand over the phone, and his blue gaze ran over her. She knew she must look awful, in her old T-shirt, with her hair all tangled, clutching the newel post to keep from keeling over onto the floor.

"What are you doing out of bed?"

Her leg beat out a dull throb of pain with every pulse of the blood through her veins. She clutched the newel post a little tighter. "I heard the phone ring. I was worried it might be—"

"It's your mother. She says she's just spoken to your father."

She reached for the phone.

"Let's get you off that leg first." He spoke into the mouthpiece. "Erica? Can you hold on just a moment more? Thanks."

And then he wrapped his arm around Natalie's waist. She could have died, he felt so warm and strong and solid. "Come on. Back to bed." He helped her to return to the bedroom, where he hoisted her onto the bed and gently positioned her broken leg on the pillows. Then, when she was all settled, he handed her the phone.

She pasted a smile on her face and hoped it would carry over into her voice. "Hi, Mom. It's me."

"Oh, Nat. How *are* you? Rick says you had an accident."

"I'm all right, Mom. Really."

"What happened?"

"I broke my leg. But it's just a hairline fracture. The doctor says in six weeks I'll be just fine."

Erica made a low sound of distress. "I should be there."

"No. No, you shouldn't. I'm fine. Really. Rick says you talked to Dad."

"Yes."

"How is he?"

"I'm not really sure, to tell you the truth. He said I wasn't to worry." A high, slightly frantic laugh escaped her. "Can you believe that? Everyone thinks he murdered Monica Malone, and I'm not to worry...."

"Where was he, when you talked to him?"

"Back at the estate. Evidently Sterling had come for him. Some place in Wisconsin, I think. Sterling convinced him to come back and talk to the police."

Natalie's stomach tightened. "He's talked to the police?"

"Yes. He's been at the police station. Being questioned. For several hours."

"Did they charge him with anything?"

"No—not yet, anyway. After the questioning was over, Sterling took Jake back to the estate. And Sterling called me from there, to say Jake was safe. I insisted he let me talk to your father. When Jake came on the line, well, it was just so difficult to make sense of what he said. He insisted that he didn't kill anyone, no matter how bad the whole thing looks. He asked me to call all of you kids. To tell you he was innocent. And then he...asked about you. About what you'd said to the police. What could he have meant by that, do you think?"

"It's all right, Mom. Don't worry."

"Don't *worry*?"

"Settle down. I'll call him and clear it all up with him right away."

"I don't see what you can clear up...."

"Mom. I'll take care of it."

"Well. All right. But are you sure you don't want me to come on over there?"

"No, Mom. I'll be fine. I promise you. I'll call you tomorrow." Natalie said goodbye before her mother could protest any further. With Rick looking on grimly, she dialed the number at the estate. But no one answered. Instead, the machine there picked up after the first ring and her father's recorded voice asked her to leave a message.

"Dad," she said into the phone, "it's me. Nat. I just spoke with Mother. I know it's late, but if you're there...?" She let the question trail off on a sigh. "Call me, Dad. Please." She turned off the phone and handed it to Rick.

"What's happening?"

Briefly she explained what her mother had told her. Then she wondered aloud, "Maybe I should go over there."

Rick was shaking his head before she even finished the sentence. "No way. Your leg's broken, Natalie. It's two in the morning. You need rest. And you're going to get it. Now."

"But if he's—"

"You're not going to run to your father's rescue, Natalie. Not tonight, anyway. Tonight, you're going to get some—" The ringing of the doorbell cut Rick off. "Who the hell is that?"

Natalie started to swing her good leg off the bed.

"Stay," Rick said, as if he were talking to Bernie.

"Rick, I have to—"

"You stay here. I'll get it."

He rose from the edge of the bed and left before she could say another word, closing the bedroom door firmly behind him.

But he stuck his head in again two minutes later. He didn't look happy. "Someone to see you."

Before she could ask who, he pushed the door all the way open. Her father stood behind him in the doorway.

Fifteen

Jake stepped around Rick and into the bedroom. "Hello, Nat."

"Dad," she said softly, thinking he looked terrible, even though his clothes were clean and it appeared that he'd showered and shaved not too long ago. Still, his eyes were puffy and red, his skin looked gray and his hair was mussed, the way it had been last night, as if he'd been forking his hands through it in agitation.

He turned to Rick. "I'd like to speak to my daughter alone, please." His voice held only a scratchy echo of its old command.

Rick crossed his arms over his broad chest, the gesture clearly indicating he wasn't going anywhere. But when he spoke, it was gently. "I think it's better that I stay."

Jake tried leveling a frozen glare at Rick. But Rick only gazed back at him, unmoved.

Natalie spoke up. "It's okay, Dad. He knows... everything that I know. He was there when I talked to Sterling."

Jake swore under his breath. "Fine. All right. Whatever." He turned from Rick, who remained near the door, and approached the bed. "What happened to your leg?"

"I broke it. Slid down the porch roof. But it's not too bad. A month and a half and I'll be running up and down the stairs again."

"Good. Good." He stood looking at her rather blankly

for a moment. And then he sighed. "Nat." He dropped heavily to the side of the bed, jarring her leg and making her wince. "I'm sorry, Nat. For everything. But I didn't do it. I really didn't. You know that, don't you?"

"Yes," she said, and meant it. Her father hadn't murdered anyone. She knew it in her bones.

"I don't really remember what I said last night, Nat. But I...I was confused, you know?"

"Yes, Dad. I know. I understand."

"Sterling says all you told the police was that you found me drunk in the library and helped me up to my rooms."

"Yes, that's what I told them."

"Good." He patted her hand. And then he bent close. His breath smelled like an open bottle of Scotch. She did her best not to recoil. "I explained to the police that I argued with Monica Malone last night. That's all that happened, Nat."

"I know. You told me."

"So if the police come snooping around you again, you might have to admit that much. I hope that's all you'll ever say."

She looked steadily into his bloodshot eyes. "Of course it's all I'll ever say. After all, it's all I know."

Her father blinked. "Yeah. That's right. It's all you know. I was drunk. I mentioned to you that I'd had an argument with Monica Malone. You took me to my rooms."

"Exactly."

"Well. Good, then." He moved as if to rise.

She caught his hand before he could get away. "Dad, you look so tired."

"I'm all right."

She tried to speak brightly. "I have an idea. Why don't you go upstairs? Take my room, get a little rest...."

But he was already pulling away, rising to his feet. "No. Can't. Gotta go."

"But, Dad—"

"I'm sorry, Nat. What a damn mess. Really sorry. Gotta go." He turned and left.

She sent a pleading glance at Rick just as Jake disappeared down the hall. "He shouldn't be driving...."

"Stay there. I'll see that he's all right." Rick followed after Jake.

Natalie listened. She heard a car start up outside. Rick returned before she could drag herself out of the bed again.

"What the hell are you doing?" He was beside her in three long strides.

"I heard a car start up. Is he—?"

Gently he pushed her back among the pillows. "Relax. He's not driving. He got into the back seat of a limousine. There was someone else at the wheel."

"Edgar, probably. That's his head chauffeur."

Rick shrugged. "The point is, he's not going to kill himself or anyone else by trying to handle a car right now."

She shook her head. "He looks so terrible."

Rick nodded. "Yeah."

"I wish I could..."

"What?"

She gave a little shrug. "I don't know. Make it all better. Make everything right."

He raised the sheet and settled it over her. "Well, you can't."

"Yeah. I know."

Her phone was on the nightstand. "I'll put that back upstairs again."

She snatched it up before he could get to it, and clutched it to her chest. "No. Leave it here. That way, if it rings, it won't bother you."

"Won't it lose its charge, without the base?"

"Rick. Leave it here."

"I want you to sleep."

"I want *you* to sleep."

They glared at each other, and then they both smiled.

He went to the door. "Good night," he said softly. He stepped into the hall, pulling the door shut behind him.

She stared at the closed door. "Good night," she whispered in return.

The next morning, Natalie hobbled into the downstairs bathroom first thing, and then refused to leave it until she'd managed to have a bath.

Rick tapped on the door as she was letting the water run. "Need some help in there?"

"No, thank you."

It took well over an hour, but when she emerged from the bathroom, every inch of her was fresh and clean.

Just after they finished breakfast, Natalie's intrepid aunt Rebecca arrived with Gabe Devereax, the private investigator the family had originally hired to look into the plane crash that had caused Grandma Kate's death.

They explained that they'd been over to the estate but Jake had still been in bed when they got there. Gabe, a rugged, powerfully built man with a take-charge air about him, said they were going to have to see about getting some decent security over there. The reporters were already swarming at the gates. It wouldn't take them long to figure out how easy it would be to get in from lakeside.

The red-haired Aunt Rebecca rolled her eyes. "Gabe's big on security."

Gabe cast her a grim glance. "Your father won't be happy when they start crawling in the windows, let me tell you." He turned to Natalie, who was sitting in the easy chair, with her leg on the pillow-stacked ottoman. "I understand that you were there, at the estate, the night that Monica Malone was killed."

Natalie knew what was going on then. Gabe and Rebecca were "on the case," trying to find out anything Natalie might know about the night of the murder.

"Yes, I was there."

"Did you speak with Jake that night?"

Natalie told them the same story she'd told the police.

"And what else?" Gabe asked.

Natalie met his probing gaze without wavering. "That's everything."

Just then, the front doorbell rang. Rick went to answer it, and Gabe and Rebecca shared a pointed glance.

"Are you sure you aren't leaving anything out?" Gabe asked quickly, before whoever was at the door could interrupt them.

"It's all I know," Natalie replied.

Erica, with Rick right behind her, appeared from the central hall. "I'm here to fuss over my daughter," she declared.

After she hugged Natalie, Rick got her a cup of coffee and made sure she was comfortable in the other easy chair.

Natalie tried not to be obvious about it as she watched the interplay between Rick and her mother. Rick had a way of putting people at ease. Her whole family had seemed to accept him without question right from the start, as if he'd always been one of them. And Erica, who was so aloof with most people, seemed to have chosen Rick as someone she could lean on, just the way she leaned on Natalie.

Natalie found herself wondering again how she ever could have thought of him as being like the other men she'd known. He was at least as good at taking care of others as she herself was. And she was truly ashamed of how badly she'd misjudged him—and painfully aware of what a fool she'd been every step of the way with him.

"Have you seen Toby?" Rick asked when he returned to the great room after seeing their visitors to the door.

Natalie shook her head. "I think he wandered outside about half an hour ago."

It didn't take Rick long to find his son.

He made a circuit of the front yard and the backyard, then went out to the dock. He heard the small voice through the open window of the boathouse.

"And everything is just fine here, even though it's very, very wet and sometimes dark, deep down the way it is...."

Rick peeked in and saw his son, near the *Lady Kate*, with what looked like a small stack of old letters beside him and one yellowed sheet of paper spread flat across his knees. Bernie sat a few feet away, listening with one ear cocked as Toby pretended to read what was written on the rumpled page.

For a moment, Rick just stood there, watching and listening, as his son babbled away. He had known for a while now that Toby would be okay, but more proof still managed to tighten his throat and put a mist of tears in his eyes.

He entered the boathouse, where the water lapped softly and the *Lady Kate* waited.

"What have you got there, son?"

Toby looked up from the page. "Letters from the friendly monster of the lake. Come look, Daddy."

Rick crouched beside his son and picked up one of the envelopes. It was addressed to Benjamin Fortune. The return address was in Sussex, England; the letter had been postmarked more than twenty years before.

Rick glanced at the stack of similar envelopes that sat on the boathouse floor between him and his son. "Where did you get these, Toby?"

Toby took his hand and pulled him over near a far wall, where he pointed at a loose floorboard. Rick bent and pried the thing up. Beneath the board was a metal-lined compartment.

"You found them in here?"

Toby nodded. "The friendly monster must of left them."

Rick grinned. "I don't know if monsters write letters."

Toby stood firm. "*Friendly* monsters do."

Rick decided not to argue. "Maybe so. But I think Natalie would probably like to see them."

Toby shrugged. "Okay."

They scooped up the rest of the letters and took them all into the house.

Natalie looked up, a relieved smile breaking across her face, when they entered the great room. "There you are I was getting a little nervous, I have to tell you." Then she frowned. "What is it?"

Rick carried the letters to her chair and handed them over.

By the time Natalie had finished reading them all Toby had lost interest in the yellowed sheets from th friendly monster of Lake Travis. He and Bernie were out in the backyard, playing fetch.

Natalie glanced up from the last letter and over at Rick, who was sitting on the sofa, a few feet away.

He asked, "Well?"

"Oh, Rick…" She hardly knew where to begin.

"What?"

"I… These letters are from someone named Celia Simpson, in England. They mention a daughter named Lana—my grandpa Ben's daughter, by this Simpson woman. From what I can read between the lines here, Celia raised Lana as her husband George's child. And it looks like Grandpa Ben wanted to know Lana—but Celia didn't want him interfering in the life she'd made for herself with her husband. So she kept Grandpa Ben at bay." She looked down at the letters again. "There's also a mention of a granddaughter, Jessica, in the last of the letters, dated about fifteen years before my grandfather's death. The granddaughter would be just a few years younger than me."

Rick stood from the couch. "Jessica, you said?"

"Yes."

"Remember the woman who called two weeks ago?"

Natalie did remember. "Jessica Holmes."

"And she called from England."

Natalie bit her lower lip. "It's probably just a coincidence, don't you think?"

Rick didn't seem to think so at all. "Did you happen to write her number down?"

Natalie shook her head.

Rick suggested carefully, "We could try London information."

After a moment, she nodded. "All right."

Rick went to the phone as Natalie busied herself putting the letters back in their envelopes and retying the twine that had held them together.

Rick spoke to her from over by the phone. "Information shows a Jessica Holmes and a J. Holmes. Should I try them?"

Ambivalent, but knowing he was right, she made a face at him. "Go for it."

Ten minutes later, they'd learned that J. Holmes was a man. And Jessica wasn't home. She did have an answering machine, though. Rick left a brief message.

"It's the best we can do, for now," he said, once he'd hung up. He looked at the stack of old letters, now tied up neatly in Natalie's lap.

"What will you do with them?"

"I'll turn them over to Sterling, next time I see him. He'll have them checked out." She set them on the table beside her.

When she turned back to Rick, he was studying her. "Why the long face?" he asked.

"Oh, I don't know...."

"You do." He sat on the end of the couch, near her chair. "Tell me."

She couldn't help but open up to him. "It's just, well, those letters mean that my grandpa Ben might have betrayed Grandma Kate."

"And you don't like to think of him that way."

"No, I don't. And it gets worse, because those letters bring to mind the ugly stories about Grandpa Ben and Monica Malone. Could there have been truth to them, too?"

"Right now, there's no way to know."

"Oh, Rick. To me, Grandpa Ben was a sweet man who took me fishing. Who listened to me. Who paid attention to me when there were so many more interesting kids in the family he could have spent his time with.''

"He was good to you.''

"Yes.''

"And he wasn't perfect.''

"Apparently not.'' She glanced over at the letters again. "I have this problem, Rick.''

"Yeah?''

"I used to look at the world through rose-colored glasses. Everyone said so. Lately, I've been trying to get real about things, you know?''

He made a sound of understanding.

"But I've kind of...botched that up, too.''

"How?''

"Well...''

"How?''

"With you. I judged you *too* harshly. I ruined everything between us.'' She waited, half hoping he'd jump in and tell her that there was still hope for the two of them.

But he didn't. He only waited for her to go on.

She bit her lip and told herself for the hundredth time to stop wishing for what was never going to be.

Rick was still thinking of Grandpa Ben. "Do you believe your grandfather loved you?''

"I have no doubt that he did.''

"Then concentrate on that,'' Rick advised her. "And accept the fact that he was human—and fallible. He made mistakes. We all do.''

The day seemed to drag by. Natalie tried to reach her travel agent, to see if there was any way she could recoup some of the money she was going to lose by canceling her cruise at the last moment. But it was Sunday, and the travel agency was closed. She'd have to wait until tomorrow to see what could be done.

As they had the day before, they left the television on, hoping to hear of some breakthrough in the mystery surrounding the death of Monica Malone. There was nothing new.

But Tracey Ducet gave an interview that appeared on the noon news. She pursed her too-red mouth and blinked her false eyelashes and still managed to look like a wounded waif.

"I hate to say it," she told the reporter. "I truly do. But the whole world knows about the bad blood between Monica Malone and my family, the Fortunes." Tracey sighed. "I suppose the police already have an idea of who did it. It's a tragedy. It truly is...."

Natalie grabbed the remote and turned it off. If she hadn't, she might have thrown one of her crutches through the screen.

"Come on," Rick said after that. "Let's blow this joint."

"What is that supposed to mean?"

"Let's get Toby and Bernie and some sandwiches and go out on the lake.

Natalie opened her mouth to say no.

Rick didn't let her get the words out. "There's a radio and a television right on the *Lady Kate*. And I'll call your mother with the number of my cell phone, in case anyone just has to get in touch with you."

"But—"

He was already headed for the pantry.

Half an hour later, Natalie found herself sitting on deck, her leg propped in front of her, eating an impromptu lunch of crackers and cheese.

It was a hot day, and the sun made bright jewels on the water. Natalie looked over the rail, remembering that first day when Rick and Toby had come to stay at Lake Travis. Only three weeks had passed since then.

Yet Natalie felt as if she'd known Rick and his son her whole life.

Soon enough, just as they had that other day, Toby and Bernie fell asleep on the deck.

It was quiet. Natalie sat sideways on the padded bench with her bad leg stretched out in front of her. Idly, as she listened to the soft lapping of the waves against the boat, she toyed with the rosebud charm that hung around her neck. Rick emerged from the cabin, where he'd disappeared a few minutes before. He came and sat on the section of bench at her back.

She put her hand on the rail and twisted her body around a little, so that she could see him. He was bending over the side.

She smiled. "What are you looking for?"

She knew his answer before he uttered it: "The friendly monster of Lake Travis."

She watched him from her awkward vantage point, her heart breaking as the full truth came to her: She was totally and completely in love with him. He'd lived in her house for less than a month—and she hadn't the faintest idea how she'd survive when he and Toby returned to their real home.

Yet she'd have to find a way. She *would* lose them, soon enough.

"Look," Rick said softly. "Can you see him?"

Biting back the tears, Natalie played along, gripping the rail a little tighter and ignoring the twinge in her leg as she craned over the side.

"Well?" he asked. "Do you see?"

"I can't...um..."

"Sure you can."

She raised her eyes from the mossy depths below them. He was right there. Looking at her.

"Oh, Rick..."

She burst into tears.

He reached for her. "Nat..."

She batted him off.

"Come here," he said, so tenderly. And that time, when he reached out, she allowed him to pull her back, across his lap.

He produced a handkerchief. She grabbed it, blew her nose and blotted up the tears. And then, at last, she simply lay there, in the one place she most wanted to be: Rick Dalton's arms.

"I messed up," he said.

"*You* messed up? No..."

"Yes. Be quiet. Let me say this."

She gulped. "All right."

"I was way too hard on you, the other night. I knew that you'd been used one time too many. And I should have gone easy. But I didn't. I wanted you. So I pushed things too far, too fast."

"No, really—"

"Are you going to let me finish?"

"All right. Yes. Okay."

"I could have been gentler, afterward, when you had all those doubts. But I have a few grim memories of my own, and they got the better of me."

"Your wife, you mean?"

He nodded. "She...jumped to conclusions a lot. And there was no talking to her, once she'd made up her mind."

"Just like me."

He brushed the hair back from her face with a caressing hand. "Still, I could have been more patient. But I wasn't. Last night, after you told me you were sorry about the things you'd said, I admitted to myself that I didn't want it to be over between us."

Natalie stared at him, happiness welling up inside her.

He wasn't through. "I made a promise to myself that I was going to do it right this time."

"Oh, Rick—"

"Wait."

She pressed her fingertips over her own lips. "All right. Sorry. Go on."

"I promised myself that I would take it more slowly, give you all the time you needed to see that I'm someone you can rely on to take care of you—every bit as much as I know that you'd always be there to take care of me."

She couldn't keep quiet a second longer. "Rick, you've shown me. I see it. Believe me, I know the truth now."

"No, I'm still pushing too fast."

"No, really, you're not. Not at all."

He shook his head. "I fell in love with you the first moment I saw you. From behind. With that lampshade on your head. And I can't wait any longer."

Natalie grabbed his hand and pressed her lips into his palm. "May I say what I want to say now? Please?"

He laughed. "All right. Go ahead."

She entwined her fingers with his. "It seems to me as if I've spent my whole life waiting for you to come along. I guess I kind of got tired of waiting. I started to...not believe anymore, that you would come. I settled in with Joel—settled *for* Joel is more like it. Do you know what I mean?"

"I think so."

"And then, when things looked bleakest, there you were. But I'd already decided you weren't coming, so I wouldn't let myself believe you had arrived at last."

He tipped his head to the side. "You know, if you married me, your life would be so much simpler."

Natalie looked into his blue, blue eyes, feeling as shimmery and weightless as the sunbeams that danced on the waters of the lake. Even her fears for her father couldn't dim the beauty of a moment like this one.

She played along with his teasing. "How would my life be simpler, if I married you?"

Rick squeezed her hand. "If you married me, we could go on a honeymoon without having to find a renter who'll take care of the dog."

She felt for the rosebud talisman around her neck, realizing that Grandma Kate had known exactly what she was doing, after all. "You're right."

He kissed the tip of her nose. "But you know us— we'll figure out a way to take Bernie along."

"And Toby, too."

"Right. What would our lives be, without the kid and the dog?"

"Not nearly so full as they're going to be."

"So. Will you marry me?"

There wasn't a doubt in her mind. Anymore. "You know I will."

"I love you."

"And I love you."

"Can I kiss you?"

"Please. Yes. Kiss me now."

Rick's lips settled against hers. Natalie wrapped her arms around his neck and kissed him back with all of her heart.

* * *

Kate lowered her binoculars.

Joy, sweet and fierce, was moving through her, giving her back some of the strength that so much recent treachery had leached away.

Dear Natalie had found happiness at last. And Kate was satisfied.

Of course, Sterling would be furious with her if he knew that she was out here. But he *wouldn't* know.

And she'd needed this, to see this. To see love triumph in a world where—she had little doubt now—her oldest son would soon be arrested and charged with the murder of Monica Malone.

Kate put away the binoculars and turned the patio boat for a secret cove she knew of. It was time she got back to Minneapolis and prepared herself for the ordeal to come.

* * * * *

FORTUNE'S CHILDREN

continues with
MYSTERY HEIRESS
by Suzanne Carey
Available in March

Here's an exciting preview...

Mystery Heiress

Stephen Hunter strolled the curving paths of St. Paul, Minnesota's Como Park Zoo. He had no kid to delight with his undivided attention, no inquisitive eight-year-old boy to whom he could explain that giraffes ate treetops for lunch.

To be gut-wrenchingly precise, he had no *David*. Instead of his cherished towheaded son, he had a gaping hole in his heart.

He knew he should start fresh. Live again, instead of simply going through the motions. He just wasn't sure how to start. He was paralyzed by the prospect of committing to anyone. Most single women his age who weren't already mothers wanted a baby, while the thought of loving and losing another child caused panic to grip him by the throat.

So Stephen wandered through the zoo, remembering happier times. Pausing to gaze at the gorillas, Stephen noticed an attractive, dark-haired woman and a frail-looking, warmly dressed blond girl who were touring the zoo. The woman's roses-and-cream complexion glowed as if it had been nourished by a cool but temperate climate. It was clear from the woman's demeanor that she was the girl's mother and loved her very much.

Unfortunately, to Stephen's physician eyes, her little girl didn't look at all well. To begin with, she was too thin, and her large, solemn eyes were too big for her face.

For some reason, when mother and child moved on to the sea island, Stephen followed at a slight distance. Imagining for a moment how it would be to have a family again. He supposed it was just as well they were strangers.

Jessica Holmes and her five-year-old daughter, Annabel, had just arrived from their native England and were suffering a bit of jet lag. Because of this, as well as Annie's illness, their tour of the zoo wasn't as brisk or cheerful as it might have been.

Jessica had come to Minneapolis for the wonderful treatment centers and for a miracle. Annie needed a bone marrow transplant, and Jessica had exhausted all avenues of inquiry among their relatives in England. In fact, just when she thought she had asked *all* her relatives, she discovered some papers indicating her grandmother had had an affair with an American, Benjamin Fortune, and had conceived Jessica's mother. That explained why Jessica had found no matches amongst her family—but now she had to find one long-lost American soldier who came from the Midwest.

Jessica shook those thoughts from her head and concentrated on her daughter. Annie took a bit of the spun-sugar confection, which colored her mouth a streaky pink, and ran ahead.

"Zebras, Mummy! *Zebras!*" she exclaimed. However, as she raced ahead, the child stumbled and fell to the pavement, skinning her left knee slightly.

Her mother was beside her in an instant, inspecting the damage. "Are you all right, Annie?" she demanded worriedly, attempting to brush every trace of dirt from the abrasion with a clean handkerchief.

Annie seemed willing to take the mishap in her stride.

However, "My head feels hot, Mummy," she complained.

From what Jess could tell on closer inspection, her child's large, green eyes were exceptionally bright, as if from a fever.

"Oh, baby," Jess whispered, her heart sinking as she enveloped the girl in a guilty hug. "We've got to get you back to the hotel at once."

She wasn't aware of the man's approach. As a result, she almost jumped to find him towering over them.

"Excuse me, but I'm a doctor. My name is Stephen Hunter. Is there anything I can do to help?" he asked.

He was tall and lean, with boyishly tousled, sun-bleached hair and penetrating blue eyes. His hands were neat and long fingered. They looked capable. Despite everything she'd heard about crime in American cities, she was inclined to trust him.

Still, she wasn't going to trust just anyone when it came to Annie's welfare.

With a fluid motion that wasn't lost on him, she arose. "Thanks, but not really," she declined in her cultivated British voice. "The abrasions on my daughter's knee aren't serious. However, she does seem to have caught cold. I've decided to give up on the zoo for today."

With an unmistakable air of authority, Stephen crouched to lay his wrist against the child's forehead and feel her neck with strong, gently probing fingers. Brief though it was, the latter exam caused her to wince.

"Your daughter has swollen glands and a temperature," Stephen said, gazing directly into the woman's dark-fringed eyes. "Hadn't you better take her to a doctor?"

Jess felt anger tinged with panic flow through her veins. "I would if we had one here in the U.S.," she snapped, then crumbled as Annie shivered slightly. "We just arrived from England and the weather's chillier than I expected," she added almost apologetically, drawing her daughter close. "I'm afraid Annie's cardigan isn't warm enough...."

Stephen didn't hesitate. "Here, take my coat," he insisted, shrugging off his sport jacket and wrapping it around Annie's shoulders. "Did you come by car?"

Jess nodded, overwhelmed by his take-charge manner and, now that she'd dropped her defenses, more than a little grateful.

"I'll carry her," he said.

With her mother at the tall stranger's side, Annie didn't protest when Stephen lifted her in his arms. Instead, she wrapped her arms around the blond doctor's neck and nestled against his tan oxford-cloth shirt as if she belonged there, as if she appreciated his *fatherliness.*

It was just an illusion, of course, fostered by Jess's anxiety plus the fact that Annie's father had so seldom evinced an interest in his daughter before his death.

Their little procession of three reached her rental car and, returning Stephen's coat, she dismissed him. "We'll be fine now," she told him. "Thanks for your help."

Stephen shrugged off her gratitude, telling her to take good care of Annie. He watched as they drove off. I isn't likely I'll run into them again in a city this size, he thought. Shrugging on his jacket and thrusting his hands into its pockets as he strode toward his Mercedes, he told himself it was for the best. Yet he couldn't deny hoping that fate would bring them together....

At last the wait is over...

In March

New York Times bestselling author

NORA ROBERTS

will bring us the latest from the Stanislaskis as
Natasha's now very grown-up stepdaughter,
Freddie, and Rachel's very sexy brother-in-law
Nick discover that love is worth waiting for in

WAITING FOR NICK

Silhouette Special Edition #1088

and in April
visit Natasha and Rachel again—or meet them
for the first time—in

The
Stanislaski
Sisters

containing TAMING NATASHA
and FALLING FOR RACHEL

Available wherever Silhouette books are sold.

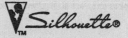

Silhouette®

In April 1997
Bestselling Author

DALLAS SCHULZE

takes her Family Circle series to new heights with

In April 1997 Dallas Schulze brings readers a
brand-new, longer, out-of-series title featuring the
characters from her popular Family Circle miniseries.

When rancher Keefe Walker found Tessa Wyndham he
knew that she needed a man's protection—she was
pregnant, alone and on the run from a heartless past.
Keefe was also hiding from a dark past...but in one
overwhelming moment he and Tessa forged a family
bond that could never be broken.

Available in April wherever books are sold.

DSST

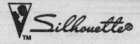

Meet the Fortunes—a family whose legacy is greater than riches. Because where there's a will…there's a *wedding!*

If you missed any Fortune's Children titles, then order now and experience the romances of the entire Fortune family!

#50177	HIRED HUSBAND (Caroline's Story) by Rebecca Brandewyne	$4.50 U.S. ☐ $4.99 CAN. ☐
#50178	THE MILLIONAIRE AND THE COWGIRL (Kyle's Story) by Lisa Jackson	$4.50 U.S. ☐ $4.99 CAN. ☐
#50179	BEAUTY AND THE BODYGUARD (Allie's Story) by Merline Lovelace	$4.50 U.S. ☐ $4.99 CAN. ☐
#50180	STAND-IN BRIDE (Michael's Story) by Barbara Boswell	$4.50 U.S. ☐ $4.99 CAN. ☐
#50181	THE WOLF AND THE DOVE (Rachel's Story) by Linda Turner	$4.50 U.S. ☐ $4.99 CAN. ☐
#50182	SINGLE WITH CHILDREN (Adam's Story) by Arlene James	$4.50 U.S. ☐ $4.99 CAN. ☐

(limited quantities available)

TOTAL AMOUNT	$
POSTAGE & HANDLING ($1.00 for one book, 50¢ for each additional)	$
APPLICABLE TAXES*	$_____
TOTAL PAYABLE	$_____

(check or money order—please do not send cash)

To order, send the completed form, along with a check or money order for the total above, payable to Silhouette Books, to: **In the U.S.:** 3010 Walden Avenue, P.O. Box 9077, Buffalo, NY 14269-9077; **In Canada:** P.O. Box 636, Fort Erie, Ontario, L2A 5X3.

Name:_____

Address:_____ City:_____

State/Prov.:_____ Zip/Postal Code:_____

*New York residents remit applicable sales taxes.
Canadian residents remit applicable federal and provincial taxes.   FCBACK6

Look us up on-line at: http://www.romance.net

Silhouette®

Don't miss these exciting titles coming to That's My Baby!—only from Silhouette Special Edition!

December 1996
CHRISTMAS BRIDE by Marie Ferrarella (SE #1069)
Could Toni D'Angelo and her ex rekindle their love? A holiday miracle made them think anything was possible—because suddenly there was a baby on the way!

February 1997
NOBODY'S BABY by Jane Toombs (SE #1081)
All Karen Henderson wanted was to find orphaned baby Danny's real father. She never dreamed she'd find a family for herself in the process!

April 1997
WHAT TO DO ABOUT BABY by Martha Hix (SE #1093)
When a handsome lawyer showed up on Carolyn Grant's doorstep with a toddler in tow, she didn't know what to think. Suddenly she had a little sister she'd never known about...and a *very* persistent man intent on making Caro his own....

THAT'S MY BABY!
Sometimes bringing up baby can bring surprises... and showers of love.

You're About to Become a *Privileged Woman*

Reap the rewards of fabulous free gifts and benefits with proofs-of-purchase from Silhouette and Harlequin books

Pages & Privileges™

It's our way of thanking you for buying our books at your favorite retail stores.

PROOF OF PURCHASE FC-PP22
Offer expires March 31, 1997

**Harlequin and Silhouette—
the most privileged readers in the world!**

For more information about Harlequin and Silhouette's PAGES & PRIVILEGES program call the Pages & Privileges Benefits Desk: 1-503-794-2499

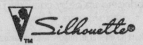